Jessica predicts the future. . . .

Patrick stood in front of Jessica and held out his hands. Jessica took them in her own hands, closed her eyes, and began to moan. She was starting to feel Patrick's energy. "Madame Jessica predicts a fight," she said. Her forehead wrinkled as she saw the vision more clearly. "A terrible fight."

"With who?" Patrick asked in a worried voice.

Jessica scrunched her face as she concentrated even harder. "Madame Jessica sees a girl," she said, building the suspense. "Dark hair, medium height . . . Her initials are . . . S . . . R . . ."

"Sophia, duh!" Janet said.

Jessica's eyes flew open. "Shhh!" she hissed. "You're disturbing my concentration."

"Sophia's my girlfriend," Patrick said with a sweet smile. "We don't fight."

"She may be your girlfriend today," Jessica said ominously. "But she won't be tomorrow."

"Oh, great," Patrick said as he turned to leave. "Thanks a lot, Jessica!"

SWEET VALLEY TWINS

The Incredible Madame Jessica

Written by
Jamie Suzanne

Created by
FRANCINE PASCAL

BANTAM BOOKS
NEW YORK • TORONTO • LONDON • SYDNEY • AUCKLAND

To Bradley Scott Halpern

RL 4, 008-012

THE INCREDIBLE MADAME JESSICA
A Bantam Book / January 1996

Sweet Valley High® and Sweet Valley Twins® are
registered trademarks of Francine Pascal

Conceived by Francine Pascal

Produced by Daniel Weiss Associates, Inc.
33 West 17th Street
New York, NY 10011

Cover art by James Mathewuse

One

Yawn! Jessica Wakefield could feel her eyelids getting heavy. She glanced over her shoulder at the alarm clock on her night table. Yikes! It was almost midnight! Jessica could hardly believe that a *book* had kept her up so late.

But it wasn't just *any* book, Jessica thought as she closed the cover and held it to her chest. It was a book on real-life psychics.

The chapter she'd just finished was about a woman named Britta Hanes, who worked with the police to solve crimes. Britta would just be sitting there eating her Corny-O's one morning and suddenly she'd get this vision of a crime. She'd see the whole thing play out in her head in detail. The only thing the police had to do was to figure out where the crime was taking place. Then they could get there and arrest the criminal.

Reading about Britta gave Jessica the goose bumps.

Now there's a psychic who gets some respect, Jessica thought admiringly.

Jessica had always felt she'd been blessed with a special psychic vision herself. Every now and then she got visions just like Britta's. Well, maybe not *exactly* like Britta's, she admitted. She'd never seen a crime. But she certainly saw other things. Things that really happened later!

The problem was, no one took Jessica's visions seriously. If they even believed her at all, they said it was coincidence. But it wasn't. Jessica was psychic. She could feel it. And one day she'd prove it to the world.

"Ah ha!" Jessica cried with delight as she watched her twin sister, Elizabeth, pour herself a bowl of Corny-O's. "I knew you were going to have Corny-O's for breakfast today!"

Elizabeth laughed. "That's because I always have cereal for breakfast. And Corny-O's is the only cereal we have in the pantry."

"I'm going shopping after work today," Mrs. Wakefield said from the stove, where she was flipping pancakes. "Make sure cereal's on the list and I'll pick up several different boxes."

Jessica grabbed a plate from the cupboard and helped herself to two golden-brown pancakes from the plate Mrs. Wakefield was piling them on. Then she took her breakfast over to the table.

"I knew you were going to have Corny-O's before I even came downstairs," Jessica said as she sat down beside her sister.

She plopped a chunk of butter onto her pancakes

and then squeezed circles of syrup over them. "I was reading this book about psychics last night before bed. Did you know some of them work with the police to try and catch criminals?"

"Sure," Elizabeth replied between spoonfuls of cereal. "Amanda Howard wrote about a psychic in one of her mysteries."

"I'm not talking about fiction, Elizabeth. I'm talking about real life." Jessica took a bite of pancake. "I was thinking I should do that," she continued. Her mouth was still half full. "You know, use my powers to help out the police."

Elizabeth raised an eyebrow. "Your powers?"

Jessica swallowed. "My *psychic* powers!" she exclaimed. "Remember when you were trapped in that stairwell at the Regent Hotel and I got that psychic vision of where you were? I saved your *life*, Elizabeth! How could you have forgotten?"

Elizabeth smiled. "I haven't forgotten," she replied. "But Jessica, you knew I went to the Regent Hotel that night. When I didn't return, it was only natural that you assumed something was wrong."

Jessica sighed. It figured that Elizabeth would try to come up with some rational explanation.

Though Jessica and Elizabeth were identical twins, they were as different as night and day. Jessica was the outgoing one. She was known for her off-the-wall ideas. She was into parties and excitement, and she loved being the center of attention. She belonged to the Unicorn Club, which was made up of girls who considered themselves to be the prettiest and most popular at Sweet Valley Middle School.

Elizabeth was pretty enough and popular enough

to belong to the Unicorns, too, but it wasn't her thing. Unicorn meetings consisted of talk about boys, clothes, movie stars, and soap operas. Elizabeth was into more serious things like reading and writing. She was editor of the sixth-grade newspaper, the *Sweet Valley Sixers*, which she had helped start. And she preferred to spend her Friday and Saturday nights curled up with a mystery or sleeping over at a friend's house and having long, serious discussions deep into the night.

But you'd never know all that if you looked at them. On the outside, Jessica and Elizabeth looked exactly alike. They both had long sun-streaked blond hair, blue-green eyes, and a dimple in the left cheek. The only way people could tell them apart was by their hair. Elizabeth tended to wear her hair pulled back in a ponytail or held with barrettes. Jessica, on the other hand, always left her hair long and flowing.

"If you don't believe I'm psychic, let me try it again," Jessica said. She placed her second and third fingers against her temples and waited for a vision to come to her. It was getting clearer. "I see our brother, Steven," she said mysteriously. "It looks like he's eating."

"So what's new?" Elizabeth snorted.

Jessica glared at her. "I'm not finished yet," she snapped. She placed her fingers against her temples again. "Steven's eating breakfast. He's having pancakes, so it's probably this morning. And it looks like he's eating . . . nine pancakes," she said confidently.

"*Nine* pancakes?" Elizabeth and Mrs. Wakefield cried at the same time.

Jessica shrugged. Steven was fourteen and a freshman at Sweet Valley High. Nine pancakes was a lot, even for him, but Jessica was sure she was right. You couldn't argue with a psychic vision as clear as hers.

"You'll see," she said with a twinkle in her eye.

"All right! Pancakes," Steven said as he came into the kitchen. His brown hair was still dripping from the shower. He set his backpack and his basketball on the floor and went to the stove.

Jessica glanced knowingly at Elizabeth. Elizabeth grinned back.

"So, how many pancakes do you think you'll eat today, Steven?" Elizabeth asked casually.

"I'll start with these," Steven replied as he grabbed the entire plate of pancakes that Mrs. Wakefield had set by the stove. There were five pancakes on the plate.

Jessica and Elizabeth watched as he devoured the whole stack in about two minutes.

"What are you two looking at?" Steven asked, his mouth full of pancake.

"Nothing," Jessica replied. "Would you like some more pancakes?" she asked sweetly.

"Now that you mention it, I think I would like a couple more," Steven said. "Are there any more, Mom?"

"I've got a couple that are ready to come off the griddle right now. Why don't you bring your plate over," Mrs. Wakefield said.

Steven ate those two pancakes, and then he ate two more.

"What did I tell you?" Jessica crossed her arms over her chest smugly. "Nine pancakes!"

Elizabeth shook her head in disbelief. "That is truly amazing," she said.

"Thank you," Jessica said as she crossed her arms. She was pleased that for once her psychic abilities weren't going unnoticed.

"Well, it *was* amazing that you guessed exactly how many pancakes Steven would eat, Jess," Elizabeth said generously. "But I was actually talking to Steven. How in the world did you manage to put away nine pancakes?"

Jessica frowned. She did all the work, but Steven got all the attention.

Steven leaned back in his chair and let out an incredibly loud burp. "I'm a growing boy," he said.

"You're a *disgusting* boy," Jessica said.

"So what's this about Jessica guessing how many pancakes I was going to eat?" Steven asked.

"It wasn't a guess," Jessica said. "It was a psychic vision!"

"Sure it was," Steven said. He ruffled Jessica's hair as he stood up. "Actually I think I'll have just one more pancake. For the road."

"Are you sure you can eat another one?" Mrs. Wakefield asked doubtfully.

"Sure," Steven replied. "We can't have Jessica's stupid predictions coming true, now, can we?"

Jessica glared at her brother. "It doesn't count," she said. "I said he'd eat nine pancakes, and he was ready to stop at nine before he knew about my vision."

Steven grabbed one more pancake and held it in his hand. He came over to Jessica and bit into it right in front of her face. Then he picked up his backpack and basketball and headed out the door.

"He probably won't even eat the whole thing,"

Jessica grumbled. "He'll probably toss it in the garbage can on his way to school."

But that was OK because Jessica knew the truth. She was psychic. And she had a feeling that pretty soon, everybody in Sweet Valley would know it, too.

"Unbelievable!" Elizabeth cried as she stared at the computer catalogue in the school library.

Ms. Luster, the librarian, put her finger to her lips. "What's the problem, Elizabeth?" she asked softly.

"Sorry." Elizabeth lowered her voice. She hadn't meant to talk so loud in the library, but she was frustrated. "I wanted to do my social studies paper on how computers have changed our lives, but practically every book on computers is checked out."

"That's too bad," Ms. Luster said sympathetically.

"And it's not just that the books are checked out. A lot of them are overdue," Elizabeth continued. "Like this one, *Computer Use in the Home*. It was due way back in October. If the person hasn't brought it back by now, do you think they ever will?"

"I don't know," Ms. Luster replied. "I'm kind of hoping we'll see a few of those overdue books again once the school fair opens."

"The school fair?" Elizabeth wrinkled her forehead. "What school fair?"

Ms. Luster motioned for Elizabeth to follow her. She went back behind the checkout desk and pulled out a yellow sheet of paper. "These notices are going to be passed out at the end of the day. You can take one now, if you'd like."

Elizabeth read the paper out loud. "Help raise money for the school library. Come to the Sweet

Valley Middle School Fair! Where: the old fire station building downtown. When: the first three Saturdays in April." Surrounding the words were pictures of balloons, cotton candy, and smiling faces. Elizabeth glanced up at Ms. Luster. "This looks great. Will all the money that's earned go to help the library?"

Ms. Luster nodded. "After we cover the expenses of the fair. I hope we'll earn a lot. Every year we get a little less money from the government to buy books for the library. And every year the prices of books go up. I want to replace some of the books that have been lost, plus buy some new ones. I was even hoping to buy some computer reference books on CD, but that may be just a dream."

Elizabeth brightened at the thought of the library getting more computer reference materials. Her family had a computer at home, so she knew how much nicer it was to be able to look things up there rather than rely only on regular books. The sound and extra pictures made things so much easier to understand.

"We're also going to have a library amnesty booth at the fair," Ms. Luster went on.

"What's that?" Elizabeth asked.

"It means kids can drop off their overdue library books and not pay a fine, no matter how late the book is," Ms. Luster explained. "Each book that gets returned means one less book we have to replace. Books are expensive, you know."

"They sure are," Elizabeth said. She knew *how* expensive because she spent a good portion of her allowance on them. She never had enough to buy all the books she wanted, though. So she depended on the library to get some of them.

Wow. I never stopped to think that the library has only so much money to spend on books, too, Elizabeth thought. *And the library had to spend a lot of that money on nonfiction books so that kids can do reports. When kids check out books for their reports and then never return them, the library has to replace them, which means less money for books like Amanda Howard mysteries.*

"There has to be something we can do to get kids to bring back their overdue library books," Elizabeth said. "Something more than just telling them they don't have to pay a fine."

"If you've got any ideas, I'd love to hear them," Ms. Luster said.

Elizabeth tapped her pencil as she tried to think of something. "Well, what if we offer a prize to the person who returns the most overdue book?" she asked. "That might motivate kids to look harder for books. Or it might make them feel less embarrassed about returning a *really* overdue book."

Ms. Luster smiled. "That's a good idea," she said. "Maybe you'd like to help out with this booth, Elizabeth"

"I'd love to!" Elizabeth jumped up from her chair. "And I bet Amy and Maria would, too." Amy Sutton and Maria Slater were Elizabeth's best friends after Jessica.

"Good," Ms. Luster said. "Make sure you tell your friends about the fair, too. We'll need other booths that are a little more entertaining than a library amnesty booth if we want to get people to come to the fair."

"I'll run a full-page ad in the *Sixers* about it," Elizabeth promised. "I'm sure lots of kids will want to help." Not that there were lots of kids who cared about the library as much as Elizabeth did. But a school fair sounded like fun. Elizabeth was sure people would participate, no matter where the money was going.

Two

"I don't think earning money for more library books is really worth calling an emergency meeting for," Lila Fowler said in a bored voice. It was four o'clock, and the Unicorns were crowded around a small table at Casey's ice cream parlor.

Jessica sighed. "It's not about earning money for more library books," she explained. "It's about making sure the Unicorns' booth is the best booth at the whole fair!"

"Jessica's right," Janet Howell said.

Jessica tossed Lila a look of satisfaction. Though Lila was Jessica's best friend after Elizabeth, the two were extremely competitive. And they both tried to please Janet Howell, who was an eighth-grader and the president of the Unicorn Club.

Janet was also Lila's cousin, so she usually took Lila's side over Jessica's. But obviously Janet understood the importance of the school fair.

"The Unicorns always have the best booths at any school function," Janet went on. "We can't let the public down."

"I suppose." Lila sighed dramatically. "But the *library* fund? Couldn't they come up with a more important charity?"

"I don't think the library qualifies as a *charity*," Mandy Miller said. "But they need to get the money from somewhere to buy all those books."

"Not to mention magazines," Jessica put in. Suddenly her eyebrows knit together in a worried expression. "What if the library doesn't make enough money to renew their subscription to *Teen Dream*?"

There were sharp intakes of breath all around the table.

"Get real!" Lila said. "How much does a subscription to *Teen Dream* cost, anyway? Twenty bucks? Big deal!"

Jessica rolled her eyes. To Lila, twenty dollars *wasn't* a big deal. She was the wealthiest girl in Sweet Valley.

"Speaking of *Teen Dream*," Tamara Chase spoke up, "did you guys see the blouse the girl on this month's cover was wearing? Wasn't it gross?"

Ellen Riteman nodded her agreement. "What were the editors at that magazine thinking? Nobody wears white lace anymore!"

Janet cleared her throat as she fingered the lacy collar on her cloud-white blouse.

Ellen gasped. Her face turned bright red. "I, uh, didn't notice your blouse, J-J-Janet," she sputtered.

Tamara swallowed hard. "I think the blouse on the

magazine was way different from yours, Janet," she said.

Ellen nodded vigorously. "*Way* different!" she agreed.

"And *your* blouse looks really great on you!" Mandy said.

"Is it new?" Jessica asked Janet.

"Yes," Janet replied casually as she stirred her ice cream. "I just got it this weekend. I got it at Valley Fashions. It was in the window, which everybody knows is where they put the clothes they expect the popular girls to buy."

"That's true," Grace Oliver said. "My next-door neighbor works there, and she said the front window is reserved for the coolest clothes, the clothes that only the really popular girls would dare to wear."

"I believe it!" Ellen said.

"Hey, that gives me an idea," Mandy said. "Since we all have such great fashion sense, maybe we could set up some sort of fashion booth at the school fair! You know, show people what looks good together, what totally clashes, that sort of thing."

"That would be great for the girls," Tamara said. "But I don't think a booth like that would go over too well with the boys."

"Yeah, we need something that *everybody* will think is great," Janet said.

"What about those fabulous cookies I made a while back for Jean Voilan?" Jessica asked. Jean Voilan was on *Days of Turmoil*, Jessica's favorite soap opera. All the Unicorns were crazy about him.

"You didn't make them for Jean Voilan!" Lila cried. "You made them in home ec."

Jessica rolled her eyes. *Picky, picky!* "They got me on *Lifestyles of the French and Famous* when Jean Voilan was a guest," she explained patiently. "And you were green with envy!"

"I was not!"

"You were too!"

"Come on, you guys, let's not argue," Mary Wallace said. "Jessica's cookies *were* pretty amazing. Maybe we should think about selling them."

Jessica crossed her arms and smiled sweetly at Lila.

Lila shook her head. "I don't think so," she said. "A bunch of Unicorns in one kitchen is *not* a pretty sight!"

Janet nodded. "No way am I going to slave away in the kitchen for three weeks," she said.

Lila returned Jessica's sweet smile.

"What about that love potion we cooked up for the school carnival?" Tamara suggested. "That went over pretty well."

Love potion. That got Jessica thinking . . .

"Yeah, but who's going to fall for it again?" Janet asked.

While the other Unicorns continued to brainstorm ideas, Jessica suddenly saw a vision of herself wrapped in a beautiful garment with long, flowing scarves. The garment was purple, the color of royalty (and the official club color of the Unicorns) and Jessica was . . . foretelling the future! "That's it!" Jessica screamed, knocking her bowl of ice cream to the floor.

The other Unicorns looked at her and then laughed.

"Way to get excited about an idea, Jessica," Mandy said as she passed some napkins to her across the table.

While Jessica bent down to pick up her bowl and wipe the floor, Tamara drummed her fingers on the table. "If we can get some teachers, or maybe even Mr. Clark, to sit in our dunking booth—" she began.

"What dunking booth?" Jessica cried from under the table. She tossed the dirty napkins onto the table and scrambled into her chair. "I don't see a dunking booth in our future. Bear with me while my vision becomes clearer," she said. She closed her eyes and put her fingers to her temples. "I see . . . purple," she said in a mysterious voice. "Lots of purple."

"Jessica's right," Ellen said. "We need a special Unicorn spin."

"I know!" Mandy exclaimed. She clasped her hand over her mouth to stifle her giggles. "What if instead of water, we fill our dunking pool with . . . grape Jell-O?"

Everybody, including Jessica, burst out laughing. Jessica had to admit a pool filled with grape Jell-O was interesting. But it wasn't as great as her idea.

"Well, actually I was talking about a purple costume," Jessica said. "A purple *fortune-teller's* costume. I, of course, will be the fortune-teller. After all, I'm the one who's psychic. And you can all be my assistants."

The laughter died down. The other Unicorns stared at Jessica.

"We've already chosen our booth, Jessica," Janet said. She turned to the rest of the group. "I'll talk to Joe and see if we can borrow the dunk tank they used at the high school fair last year. It would be nice if we didn't have to build the tank, if all we had to do was fill it." Joe Howell was Janet's fourteen-year-old brother, and Steven's best friend.

"You mean you really want to do a plain old dunk tank?" Jessica asked incredulously.

"It's not going to be plain," Belinda Layton said. "It's going to be filled with Jell-O."

"That is what we agreed on when you were busy playing under the table," Janet said with a smirk.

"But what's so great about a dunk tank?" Jessica asked. "It's like something you'd see on a bad TV show. But a fortune-telling booth—"

Janet shook her head. "Forget it, Jessica," she said. "We're doing the dunk tank. Now, who wants to go shopping for Jell-O?"

Jessica crossed her arms in front of herself and fumed. Her fortune-telling booth was a much better idea than a dunking booth. People loved to know what was going to happen in the future. And she, Jessica Wakefield, had the power to tell them.

Unfortunately, as president, Janet Howell had the power to veto her.

Jessica sighed. *Maybe I should just set up a fortune-telling booth on my own, without the Unicorns*, she mused. *I could do it. I'm certainly psychic enough. The examples of my psychic abilities are just too numerous to count.*

But did Jessica really want to set up a booth all by herself? Without the Unicorns? *Well, why not?* she asked herself. After all, *she* was the one who was psychic. Why should she share the spotlight with everyone else? She could get Elizabeth to help her with some of the minor details, but for the most part, she could run the booth herself.

Janet wouldn't be happy about it, but that was too bad. There was no doubt in Jessica's mind that a fortune-telling booth was going to be way more popular than a dunk tank. The idea of all those people lining up outside *her* booth, waiting to hear *her* psychic visions, filled Jessica with excitement. She'd be the hit of the Sweet Valley Middle School Fair.

"Elizabeth Wakefield! Have I got a deal for you," Jessica announced as she slammed the front door closed.

Maybe the Unicorns didn't recognize a good idea when they heard it, but Elizabeth would. Jessica could see it now. Her booth would be so mobbed that she'd need Elizabeth to help keep the crowds under control.

Maybe Elizabeth could hand out a brief three- or four-page list of true-life examples of Jessica's psychic abilities. That way people would have something to do while they waited in line.

"Elizabeth! Where are you?" Jessica yelled. Here she was bubbling over with ideas and she couldn't even *find* her sister. She went from the kitchen to the den to the family room. "There you are!" she cried.

Elizabeth was spread out on the floor, surrounded by an assortment of bright poster paper. She grunted a greeting as she continued to outline letters in black Magic Marker.

"Guess what!" Jessica said as flopped onto the floor beside her sister. "The Incredible Madame Jessica is going to be appearing at the Sweet Valley Middle School Fair!"

"Who's Madame Jessica?" Elizabeth asked absently as she continued to outline one of her letters.

Jessica stomped her foot. "*Me*, silly! I'm going to peer into the future and tell people what I see. It's going to be totally awesome! But I'm probably going to need somebody to help control the crowds. So since you're so into the library and you probably want to see me make a ton of money for your cause, I decided *you* should be my personal assistant," she said cheerfully.

"No thanks," Elizabeth replied. "I've already signed up to work in the library amnesty booth."

"The what?" Jessica asked, scratching her head.

"The library amnesty booth," Elizabeth repeated as she started on another letter. "That's a booth where people can return their overdue books and not have to pay a fine."

"You could get out of it, couldn't you?" Jessica asked.

Elizabeth glanced up at Jessica, then lowered her eyes again to her poster. "Why would I want to?"

"Because it's boring!" Jessica cried. "My fortune-telling booth is going to be the best booth at the whole fair, Elizabeth. People are going to be lined up for miles just to hear me tell their fortunes."

"That's nice," Elizabeth muttered as she started coloring in the letters.

She wasn't even listening! Jessica frowned. "I can't believe you! Here I am, offering you the chance of a lifetime, and you totally ignore me!"

"I'm sorry. What?" Elizabeth asked as she looked up from her work.

"Never mind," Jessica said. "You stick with your library whatever booth. I'll just do my fortune-telling booth alone."

"OK," Elizabeth said cheerfully as she turned back to her poster.

Jessica threw up her hands in frustration. *I guess I'll have to do it by myself,* she decided. People always said it was lonely at the top.

"So if we can get people to return all their overdue library books, we can spend the money we earn at the fair on new books rather than on replacing old ones," Elizabeth explained at dinner that night.

"That's a good idea," Mr. Wakefield said.

"I wouldn't be surprised if you see some books that are pretty overdue," Mrs. Wakefield said as she scooped some salad into a bowl. "Offering a prize to the person who returns the most overdue book is likely to motivate people to look a little harder."

"That's what we're hoping," Elizabeth said.

"What's the prize going to be, anyway?" Steven asked as he buttered a roll.

"I'm not sure yet," Elizabeth replied.

"Just don't make it a book," Jessica said between bites of her salad. "Why would you want to return one book just to get another one?"

"Actually I was going to talk to the owner of Guido's and see if he'll donate a gift certificate for a free pizza," Elizabeth said.

Steven immediately rose from the table.

"Where are you going?" Mrs. Wakefield asked him.

He wiggled his eyebrows. "To check my room for overdue library books!"

Everybody laughed. Steven sat down.

"Well, doesn't anybody want to hear about *my* booth at the school fair?" Jessica asked.

"Of course we do," Elizabeth said. "You said earlier you're going to do something with fortune-telling."

Steven slapped his hand to his forehead. "Not that psychic stuff again!" he said.

"Yes, that psychic stuff again!" Jessica said. "Can I help it if I was born with a gift?"

"A gift for melodrama," Steven said.

"Leave her alone, Steven," Elizabeth said. "People like to have their fortunes told. I think Jessica's going to make a lot of money for the library."

Jessica's eyes sparkled. "I'm going to make more money than anybody," she predicted.

"Where's Jessica?" Lila asked.

It was Friday afternoon, and all of the Unicorns except for Jessica were walking to Sweet Valley Foods to buy Jell-O.

"She said she's too busy planning her fortune-telling booth to go shopping with us," Janet said, rolling her eyes.

"You mean she's not going to work on the Unicorn booth?" Ellen Riteman asked.

"Nope." Janet shook her head. Not that she cared. Jessica Wakefield was so full of herself. Janet could hardly believe she'd go off and set up her own booth for the school fair! Who did she think she was?

But Janet derived some satisfaction from the fact that Jessica was sure to fall flat on her face. *A fortune-telling booth! Who's going to believe that Jessica Wakefield can really look into the future?*

"Here we are," Kimberly Haver announced as they headed up the crowded parking lot. The door opened automatically, and the girls trooped into the brightly lit grocery store.

"So where's the Jell-O?" Lila asked.

"Probably over by the baking supplies," Mandy Miller responded. "Come on."

The girls passed the canned goods and headed toward the baking supplies. Janet scanned the items on the shelf as they made their way down the aisle.

"Here it is!" Tamara cried triumphantly as she grabbed a box from the shelf. "Grape Jell-O!"

Janet smiled as she thought about Mr. Clark landing in their pool of grape Jell-O. *We're going to have the best booth at the school fair,* she told herself. *And Jessica Wakefield is going to have the stupidest.*

"I wonder how much we're going to need to fill the dunking pool?" Lila asked.

"A lot," Ellen replied.

"I think Joe said the pool holds five hundred gallons of water," Janet said. "How much Jell-O does one box make?"

Tamara turned the box over and read. "Makes four half-cup servings."

"That's only two cups total," Mandy said.

"We're going to need, like, a thousand boxes of this stuff," Lila moaned.

Great, Janet thought. *Just great!*

"Wait a minute," Mary said. "Don't grocery stores have a section of larger-size servings? You know, like if you have to cook for a crowd or something?"

"It doesn't hurt to look," Janet said with hope.

They walked up and down all the aisles until

they came to one marked INSTITUTIONAL FOODS.

"Whoa! Look at this jar of pickles!" Tamara cried.

"And look at this container of ketchup!" Kimberly squealed.

"I think we've come to the right place," Janet said with a grin. She scanned the shelves carefully as they moved down the aisle.

When they reached the end, Ellen sighed. "They don't have it," she said with disappointment.

Janet frowned. She couldn't believe they sold a jar of pickles that was half as tall as she was, but no large quantities of Jell-O. "Let's look again," she said. "Maybe we missed it."

She started down the aisle again and the others followed. Janet felt her heart sinking. This was the best idea ever, and they weren't going to be able to pull it off because the stupid grocery store didn't sell huge quantities of grape Jell-O.

"Here it is!" Lila announced with delight. She held up a large white bag with red lettering that read LIME JELL-O.

Janet sighed with relief. "How much does it make?" she asked, grabbing the bag from Lila.

Janet and Lila put their heads together as they read the directions on the back. "One bag makes five gallons," Lila read.

"Yeah, but that's *lime* Jell-O," Tamara said. "I thought we wanted grape."

"I don't see any grape," Lila said. "They've got lime and strawberry. That's it."

"Well, we could get a bunch of lime and a bunch of strawberry and mix them," Mandy suggested. "Don't red and green make purple?"

"I think so," Ellen said.

"Mandy, you're a genius!" Janet exclaimed. She grabbed up every bag of strawberry and lime Jell-O the store had. "Wait a minute," she said, looking down at the five bags in her arms.

"Don't worry about how we're going to pay for it," Lila said quickly. "My dad gave me his credit card. He said he could use the tax deduction."

"That's not what I'm worried about," Janet said. She put one bag down at a time as she counted, "five, ten, fifteen, twenty, twenty five—there's still only enough Jell-O here to make twenty five gallons. We need five hundred!"

"Why don't we see if the manager is here?" Kimberly suggested. "We don't need the Jell-O for a couple weeks. Maybe they can get us enough packages by then."

The Unicorns trooped to the row of cashiers at the front of the store. "Excuse me," Lila said to the lady at checkout number one. "Is the manager in?"

The lady's name tag read SUE. Sue picked up a black phone and said in a bored voice, "Mr. Tate to register one, please. Mr. Tate to register one."

A couple minutes later, a short man with a large round stomach came over to them. "Can I help you girls?" he asked.

"Yes, we need a hundred bags of this stuff," Janet said, holding up one of the bags of Jell-O. "We need half strawberry and half lime. Unless you can get all grape?"

The man scratched his forehead. "I don't think grape Jell-O comes in bulk. But I could get you the strawberry and the lime. How soon do you need it?"

"A week from tomorrow," Janet said.

"I'll have to check with my distributor, but I can probably get it on my trucks next week. What do you need a hundred bags of Jell-O for, anyway?"

"We're going to fill our dunking tank with it at the Sweet Valley Middle School Fair," Ellen said proudly.

"A dunking tank full of Jell-O?" Mr. Tate raised an eyebrow. "Now I've heard it all."

"You should come to our fair," Tamara said. "It's going to be great!"

"Well, maybe I will," Mr. Tate said.

Three

"Ta da!" Jessica sang as she twirled into Elizabeth's room on Sunday afternoon. An armful of bracelets jangled together as she spun around, and about three feet of purple scarves trailed behind her. "What do you think?"

Elizabeth fastened her french braid with a blue scrunchie and stared at her sister.

Jessica was wearing a thin lavender blouse with puffy sleeves, a silver chain belt, deep-purple leggings, and a bunch of purple scarves draped over her shoulders.

"Is that what you're wearing to Bruce Patman's party?" Elizabeth asked. She herself was wearing a one-piece blue swim suit under a white terry cloth cover-up and blue cotton shorts. She also carried her bright yellow beach bag, which was big enough to carry her friend Sophia Rizzo's birthday present. Bruce just happened to be throwing his party on Sophia's birthday.

"Uh-huh," Jessica replied as she turned to get a view of her back in Elizabeth's mirror. "I thought I'd give everyone a preview of the Incredible Madame Jessica."

"But Jess," Elizabeth protested. "This is a *pool* party. Don't you want to go swimming?"

Jessica put her fingers to her temples. "I have a vision," she said in a low, drawn-out voice, just like the psychics on TV. "A vision of something terrible happening if I get into the pool today."

Elizabeth suppressed a giggle. "Like what?" she asked.

"I don't know," Jessica said in her normal voice. "I just would rather tell fortunes than swim."

A warning light flashed inside Elizabeth's brain. She had seen her sister get carried away with thinking she was psychic before. And usually when Jessica got carried away with things, Elizabeth somehow ended up dragged into the whole mess, too.

"What?" Jessica asked with a frown. "What are you thinking?"

Elizabeth sighed. She didn't want to hurt Jessica's feelings. "Nothing," she replied. "I just hope you know what you're doing."

"Don't I always?" Jessica asked confidently.

Elizabeth raised an eyebrow. "Actually . . ."

"Come on," Jessica broke in, gently nudging Elizabeth toward the door. "Let's go party."

"The Incredible Madame Jessica has arrived," Jessica announced dramatically as she stepped onto the pool deck out back. She tossed back her scarves as all eyes turned to her.

Bruce was the first to speak to her. "I hate to break this to you, Jessica," he said, "but Halloween is months away."

Denny Jacobson and Brian Boyd laughed.

Jessica glared at them. "For your information, I can see into the future. And what I see for the three of you is not a pretty sight."

"Oh, I'm scared," Brian said.

Jessica chose to ignore them. "I will be available for consultation at the school fair next Saturday, but if any of you would like a preview, I'd be happy to look into your future right now and tell you what I see for just one dollar!" she announced.

"A *dollar*?" Bruce asked.

"You've got to be kidding," Denny said.

"Come on." Brian punched Denny in the arm. "Is this a pool party or what?" He ran down to the pool and cannonballed into the water.

Bruce and Denny jumped in right behind him. Water sloshed up on the deck and soaked Jessica's shoes. "Hey!" she cried, jumping back. But nobody was paying any attention to her.

"Who rubbed a lamp and let you out?" Janet Howell asked as Jessica joined her and Lila on the other side of the pool.

"I'm not a genie," Jessica said indignantly. "I'm a *psychic*."

Lila snorted. "Could've fooled me."

Jessica smiled sweetly at Lila. "Well, that wouldn't take much, now, would it?" she said. Then she spun around in a circle. "This is my outfit for the school fair next week. What do you guys think?"

"I think you're crazy to abandon the Unicorns for such a stupid idea," Janet said as she turned her attention to the magazine in her lap.

"It's not stupid!" Jessica argued.

"Oh, come on, Jessica," Lila said. "You don't honestly think people are going to believe you're psychic, do you?"

"Of course they will," Jessica replied confidently. "I *am* psychic!"

"Yeah, right," Lila snorted. "And I'm the queen of England."

Just then, Ellen Riteman joined them. "Hey, Ellen," Jessica said. "I'm giving a preview of my fortune-telling booth today. For just one dollar, I will gaze into your future—"

"That's nice, Jessica," Ellen said quickly, dismissing Jessica with a wave of her hand. "Did you guys hear about Sally Holcomb?"

Janet glanced at Ellen over her magazine. "What about her?"

"She went out with a *high school* boy!"

"So what?" Jessica said impatiently. "That's old news. Now, about my fortune-telling—"

"Excuse me, Jessica," Janet interrupted. "But I think we're all a little more interested in Sally than we are in your fortune-telling."

Jessica crossed her arms. "Well, of course you are. You can't stand to talk about my fortune-telling because you're jealous." She tossed her scarves behind her shoulders.

"Jealous?" Janet cried. "Of you?"

"Well, sure," Jessica replied. "I'm going to have the most popular booth at the school fair."

"I doubt that," Janet said, biting her lip.

Jessica smiled secretively. She couldn't help but notice that Janet didn't look as confident as she sounded.

"How come you're doing the cooking when this is Bruce's party?" Sophia Rizzo asked her sort-of boyfriend, Patrick Morris, as he flipped a burger. Orange flames licked at the sizzling meat.

Patrick cocked his head and smiled. "Because Bruce asked me to," he replied.

Sophia glanced over her shoulder at Bruce splashing around in the pool. *How typical of him to throw a party and make someone else do all the work*, Sophia thought. *And how typical of Patrick to do the work without complaining.* He was the nicest boy she'd ever met.

"Well, let me help you," she said, reaching for the cheese. In the process, her arm brushed against Patrick's. She smiled at him and he smiled back.

Sophia's heart pounded with excitement. Today was her birthday, and so far, Patrick was acting like he didn't even know. *He must be planning something really special*, Sophia thought. *Maybe flowers? Or jewelry?*

"Hey, guys." Jessica Wakefield interrupted Sophia's thoughts. "Would you like me to tell your fortunes?" she asked.

"Sorry," Patrick said, "but I have to keep an eye on the burgers."

"Well, what about you, Sophia?" Jessica asked. "It only costs a dollar."

"A dollar!" Sophia cried. "Don't you think that's a little steep?"

Jessica looked like she was thinking it over. "Oh, all right," she said finally. "You twisted my arm. I'll do it for fifty cents."

Even fifty cents was more than Sophia was willing to pay. "Sorry, Jessica," she said. "I think I'll stay and help Patrick."

"You don't have to," Patrick said.

"I know," Sophia said with a smile. "I want to."

Jessica sighed. Then suddenly her eyes flashed. "Hey, Patrick, why don't you let me tell your fortune after everyone's eaten?"

Sophia rested a protective hand on Patrick's shoulder. "Well, it depends on what we're doing. We might be—busy."

Busy celebrating my birthday! she thought.

"Hey!" Elizabeth said as she and her sort-of boyfriend, Todd Wilkins, joined Jessica. Both held plates of food. "You having fun?"

Jessica shrugged. "I'd be having more fun if someone would let me tell their fortune. What about you, Todd? I've been charging everyone else a dollar, but I could give you a discount. I'll tell your fortune for fifty cents."

"Jessica!" Elizabeth said sharply. "This is a party. You shouldn't be charging people."

Jessica shrugged. "Everything has a price tag, Elizabeth. Do you think Bruce got all this food for free just because it was for a party? If I provide entertainment, I deserve to be paid."

"But Jessica, Bruce didn't hire you," Elizabeth pointed out.

Jessica rolled her eyes. Elizabeth could be so

exasperating sometimes! "I'm not doing this for myself," Jessica said as though she could hardly believe Elizabeth would think such a thing. "I'm doing it for *you*. I'm doing it for the *library*. If people see how great I am at fortune-telling, they'll come to my booth at the school fair next Saturday."

"Well . . ." Elizabeth said thoughtfully.

"I was even planning to turn in the money I made today to the library fund," Jessica said. Actually, it hadn't occurred to Jessica to turn in any money she made, but that wasn't a bad idea. If people thought the money was going to a good cause, maybe they'd let her tell their fortunes.

"Well, I'm afraid I don't have any money on me, Jessica," Todd said as he ran his hand through his brown hair. "So, as much as I'd like to have my fortune told, I'll have to pass."

Jessica sighed. Todd was so boring. She could hardly believe he'd go somewhere without any money. "Well, I guess I'll just have to go and find somebody who *does* have some money," she said. "See you guys later."

"Hey, Peter," Jessica called to Peter DeHaven. Peter was in Jessica's science class. "For a mere fifty cents, I will look into your future and tell you what I see."

"No thanks," Peter replied. "We're getting a volleyball game together."

"Come on," Jessica pleaded. "It won't take very long. Besides, it's not good to run around on a full stomach."

"I think that's an old wives' tale, Jessica," Sarah Thomas said.

Jessica turned. Sarah had an empty plate in her hand. Jessica smiled hopefully. "Hi, Sarah," she said. "Would you let me tell your fortune for fifty cents?"

"Not now," Sarah replied. "I want to get some watermelon."

"How about for free?" Jessica muttered as Sarah walked away. *How could these people be more interested in volleyball or food than in having their fortunes told?* Jessica wondered.

Her bracelets rattled as she plopped down on the grass in front of the volleyball game. She felt so dejected. On the other side of the court, Janet, Lila, and Ellen had their heads bent together. Suddenly they all looked over at her and laughed.

Jessica felt her cheeks burn. The Unicorns were probably talking about how nobody was interested in Jessica's fortune-telling. They probably thought her booth was going to bomb next week.

I've got to find somebody who will let me tell their fortune, Jessica thought frantically. But everybody was either playing volleyball or watching the volleyball game. Everybody except Patrick Morris. He was cleaning the grill. Jessica rose to her feet and hurried over to him.

"You said you'd let me tell your fortune after you finished with the burgers," she said with confidence.

"I did?" Patrick looked at her with uncertainty.

"Yes, you did." Jessica nodded. "And since this is really just a preview of what's to come at the school fair, I'll even do it for free. What do you say?"

Patrick nervously ran his hand through his hair.

"Well, OK," he said at last. "Just let me put this grill back together."

"You'll let me?" Jessica squealed with delight. "You'll really let me?"

Patrick grinned. "I'm not going to regret this, am I?" he asked.

"Oh, you won't regret it," Jessica promised. "Hey, everyone, listen up! I'm going to tell Patrick's fortune." She glanced around. Where should she do it? She needed just the right place. A place with ambiance. "The pool house!" she cried. "I'm going to do it in the pool house. Follow me, everyone!"

Jessica grabbed Patrick by the arm and led him to the pool house. A few of the kids who were watching the volleyball game straggled in behind them.

"Patrick's such a wimp," Brian Boyd whispered.

Yes, and thank God for that, Jessica thought as she noticed that the Unicorns had followed them into the pool house. She moved a stack of towels off of a small table and hoisted herself up on it. She crossed her legs. "Come here, Patrick. Give me your hands," she ordered.

Patrick stood in front of Jessica and held out his hands. Jessica took them in her own hands, closed her eyes, and began to moan.

"What's she doing?" Jessica heard Kimberly Haver whisper.

"I don't know," Lila Fowler responded. "Meditating?"

Jessica opened her eyes and glared in the direction of the whispers. "I must have silence!" she said. Once the whispering stopped, she closed her eyes again. She took a deep breath and slowly let it out.

She was starting to feel Patrick's energy. "Madame Jessica predicts a fight," she said. Her forehead wrinkled as she saw the vision more clearly. "A *terrible* fight."

"With who?" Patrick asked in a worried voice.

Jessica scrunched her face as she concentrated even harder. "Madame Jessica sees a girl," she said, building the suspense. "Dark hair, medium height . . . Her initials are . . . S . . . R . . ."

"Sophia, duh!" Janet said.

Jessica's eyes flew open. "Shhh!" she hissed. "You're disturbing my concentration."

"Sophia's my girlfriend," Patrick said with a sweet smile. "We don't fight."

"She may be your girlfriend today," Jessica said ominously. "But she won't be tomorrow."

"Oh, great," Patrick said as he turned to leave. "Thanks a lot, Jessica!"

Jessica only shrugged. Was it *her* fault Patrick didn't like what she had to say? She only reported what she saw. "OK," she said, clapping her hands together. "Who's next?"

Silence.

Jerry McAllister and Brian Boyd turned to leave.

"Surely *someone* else dares to look into the future," Jessica said desperately. She noticed her sister sitting in the back with Todd, Amy Sutton, and Ken Matthews. *Come on, Elizabeth.* She willed her sister to step forward.

But instead of walking over to her, Elizabeth turned to say something to Amy.

Elizabeth! You want to have your fortune told. You will

rise and come to the front of the room, Jessica thought as she stared hard at her sister.

Suddenly Elizabeth glanced up at Jessica.

Come on, Elizabeth, Jessica looked hard at her sister as Lila and Ellen stood up to leave.

"Oh, all right," Elizabeth said as she made her way to Jessica. "You can look into my future."

Jessica smiled. *At least my twin powers are working*, she thought.

Elizabeth stepped up to the table and held out her hands just like Patrick had done. Jessica took Elizabeth's hands and closed her eyes once again.

"Oh," she said with surprise. This vision was stronger than the last. Probably because she and Elizabeth were twins. It was easier to feel Elizabeth's psychic energy. But the vision wasn't good. "You're going to flunk your history test this week . . ."

Elizabeth yanked her hands away. "I will not," she said with annoyance. "I love history."

"This is bogus," Denny Jacobson said, shaking his head.

"Yeah, you're a fake, Jessica," Janet Howell said.

By this time, all the kids were turning to leave.

"No I'm not!" Jessica protested. But no one cared. They were all leaving.

"You got a Frisbee, Patman?" Todd asked.

"Yeah, check under the deck."

"My fortunes will come true," Jessica called after them. "You'll see!"

But no one paid her any attention.

Sophia checked her watch. Her mom would be coming to pick her up in about five minutes. She was sitting with Patrick under a large maple tree, and he still hadn't said anything about her birthday. In fact, he seemed a little distracted.

"So what do you think about Jessica's prediction?" he asked finally.

Sophia shrugged. "What do you think about it?"

"I don't know," Patrick said. He reached for her hand. "I don't see any reason why we should get into a fight. Do you?"

Sophia stared at the kids who were playing volleyball. She didn't know quite how to answer Patrick at that moment.

Four

There he was! The insensitive jerk! Look at him strutting down the hall with that goofy smile on his face, Sophia Rizzo thought as she watched Patrick Morris walking toward her. It was Monday morning. Her birthday had come and gone without a single word from Patrick.

Sophia slammed her locker closed.

Patrick jumped. The smile disappeared. "Sophia! What's wrong?" he asked as he held out a hand to her.

Sophia backed away. "Don't you touch me, you—you—you—cretin!" *Cretin?* she thought. She didn't know what it meant exactly, but it was the worst name she could think of on the spur of the moment. "You've got everybody thinking you're such a *nice* guy," she continued as she loomed closer to him, forcing him to take a step back. "But it's all a put-on, isn't it? Deep down you're just like any other insensitive creep!"

"What?" Patrick cried. He glanced nervously at the crowd that had formed around them. "I . . . I . . . I . . . have no idea . . . w-w-what you're talking about, Sophia. Can we go somewhere and talk?"

"No!" Sophia yelled.

"But I don't even know what I did to make you so mad," Patrick protested.

"You. Forgot. My. Birthday," she said as she punched his chest with her finger, punctuating each word.

Patrick's mouth dropped open.

"Yesterday, at Bruce's party, I waited all afternoon for you to say something or do something," she went on, her eyes becoming misty. "It didn't have to be much. Just something to show you cared."

"I do care, Sophia," Patrick said gently as he reached toward her.

Sophia backed away. She had to admit, he looked like he felt bad, but as far as she was concerned, it was too late. "Yeah, right," she spat. Spinning on her heel, she walked away as fast as she could.

"Did you hear!" Jessica squealed with delight as she hurried across the lunchroom to the Unicorner. The Unicorner was the table the Unicorns always claimed in the cafeteria. "Sophia Rizzo and Patrick Morris broke up!"

"Gee, Jessica. Don't feel bad for Sophia or anything," Lila said as she took a bite of her salad.

"Oh, I do feel bad for Sophia," Jessica said as she helped herself to a cherry tomato from Lila's salad. "But I *told* Patrick this would happen," she said smugly.

"How did you know it would happen?" Ellen asked.

"Lucky guess," Janet muttered.

"It was not!" Jessica said. "I've told you before. I'm psychic."

"Hey, Jessica!" Aaron Dallas said as he walked past the Unicorner with his tray. Aaron was Jessica's sort-of boyfriend. "That was pretty cool how you said Patrick and Sophia would break up and they did."

"What can I say?" Jessica shrugged modestly. "It's a gift."

"It's a farce," Janet snorted.

"You also said Elizabeth would flunk her history test," Lila reminded Jessica.

"So?"

"So there's no way that's going to happen," Lila said. "I'm in Elizabeth's history class, and I know for a fact she aced that test this morning. She turned in her test before anybody else."

Jessica shrugged. She knew Lila had a point. Elizabeth had never failed a test in her life—she almost never got below an A. But you couldn't argue with a vision as strong as Jessica's. "I just report what I see," she said. "And what I saw was Elizabeth flunking her test."

"Uh-huh," Janet said. "And what I see is you falling flat on your face on Saturday."

"In your dreams, Janet." Jessica tossed her hair. "Only in your dreams."

The next morning Elizabeth watched as Mr. Nydick walked up and down the rows, handing history tests back. She could tell by the smiles and high-fives that most kids had done well on the exam. Elizabeth wasn't surprised. It *was* a pretty easy test. Elizabeth sort of expected to get back a perfect paper.

Mr. Nydick was heading up her row again. He frowned as he handed Elizabeth her paper.

She gasped. There at the top of her paper was a bright red F.

Elizabeth could feel her whole body shaking. She'd never gotten an F on *any* test before, much less a history test. History was one of her best subjects. And she knew the American Revolution as well as if she'd actually lived it.

How could this have happened? Elizabeth asked herself. She stared at her paper. There was only one answer marked wrong on the first page. She flipped to the second page. There weren't any wrong on that page. *Did Mr. Nydick grade this test harder than usual or what?* she wondered.

Then she realized there was a third page. Elizabeth drew in her breath as she stared at the huge red question mark Mr. Nydick had made across the page. She hadn't noticed this third page yesterday. *Well, that explains it*, Elizabeth thought. She buried her face in her hands. *How could I have been so stupid?*

"What's the matter, Elizabeth?" Lila asked from across the aisle.

Lila wasn't one of Elizabeth's favorite people, but it was nice of her to be concerned. Elizabeth showed Lila her test score. "I guess I was in such a hurry to turn in the test, I didn't see there was a page three," she said miserably. "The pages must have been stuck together."

Lila's eyes widened in amazement. "You mean

you flunked?" she cried. "Just like Jessica said you would?"

Elizabeth blinked. "This has nothing to do with Jessica's prediction," she said. "I missed the questions on page three. That is why I flunked."

"But Jessica *knew* you were going to flunk," Lila insisted. "Maybe she really *is* psychic."

Elizabeth shook her head. "It's just a coincidence, Lila."

"I don't know, Elizabeth." Lila twirled her dark hair around her finger. "That's one *amazing* coincidence."

"Oh, Lizzie, I heard about your history test," Jessica said as she barged into Elizabeth's room after school. "I'm so sorry."

Elizabeth looked up from the article she was proofing for the next issue of the *Sixers*. Jessica was grinning from ear to ear. "Funny," Elizabeth said. "You don't look very sorry."

Jessica laughed. She plopped down on Elizabeth's bed. "I am," she insisted. "Really. But you have to admit, it *is* kind of exciting." She practically had stars in her eyes. "I haven't been wrong about a prediction yet."

Elizabeth sighed. "Jess, I didn't fail that test because you said I would. I failed it because I didn't answer the questions on page three."

"Yes, but *why* didn't you answer the questions on page three?" Jessica asked mysteriously. "You know, my power is so great that sometimes I amaze even myself!"

"I'm pretty amazed, too, Jess," Elizabeth said with a smile.

"Really?" Jessica squealed.

Elizabeth stifled a giggle. "I'm amazed that you take this psychic stuff so seriously."

Jessica stuck out her tongue and stomped through the bathroom to her own bedroom.

"You have to agree, Elizabeth, it was pretty unlikely that Patrick and Sophia would break up," Amy Sutton said. "And it was pretty unlikely that you'd flunk a history test. But Jessica predicted both things!"

Elizabeth and Amy were in the library on Thursday morning. Elizabeth thought it would be a good idea to send a special notice about the library amnesty booth to all the kids who had books that were more than a month overdue.

"Don't tell me you're getting caught up in all this Madame Jessica stuff, too," Elizabeth said as she filled out the next overdue notice.

Amy shrugged. "I don't know," she said. "All I'm saying is, it's pretty spooky."

It *was* spooky, Elizabeth had to admit. But it was a spooky *coincidence*. That was all.

She glanced toward the door just as Jerry McAllister put a book in the book drop and then turned to make a quick getaway.

"Hey!" Elizabeth cried. "Is that book you just returned overdue?"

Jerry ran his hand through his hair and grinned sheepishly. "Gee, I don't know," he said. "I didn't look."

Elizabeth grabbed the book from the book drop and opened the back cover. "Jerry, this book is *two weeks* overdue!"

"So?" Jerry shrugged.

"So, you owe a dollar in fines," Elizabeth said.

"Oh, come on," Jerry whined. "I brought the book back. I thought fines were only for people who don't bring books back at all."

"No, if you don't bring the book back at all, you have to pay for the book," Elizabeth explained. "But if the book is late, you have to pay a fine for each day you kept it past the due date."

"But I didn't read it all those days," Jerry protested.

"Yeah, and all those days you didn't read it, no one else could read it, either," Elizabeth pointed out. "Libraries depend on their patrons to bring their books back on time, Jerry."

"OK, OK," Jerry said, reaching into his front pocket. He pulled out a crumpled dollar bill and tossed it on the counter. "There. Are you happy now?"

"I would've been happier if you'd returned your book on time," Elizabeth said as Jerry walked away.

"You were pretty rough on him," Amy said softly.

Elizabeth recorded Jerry's fine in the overdue book ledger. "I'm just tired of people taking the library for granted," she said. "I mean, if everybody kept their books for as long as they wanted, how could a library survive?"

"I don't know," Amy replied. "But at least he paid. He could've just held on to the book until Saturday and then brought it back for free."

"I suppose," Elizabeth said. She didn't want to argue with Amy. But she couldn't help wondering why she should be *grateful* Jerry decided to pay his fine. After all, when you checked out a book, you had an obligation to return it on time or pay the fine.

In fact, now that she thought about it, Elizabeth wondered whether this library amnesty project was such a good idea after all. Was it good to let people off the hook so easily? What if the next time somebody had an overdue book, they decided to just hang on to it until the next time there was a library amnesty project? *What if this whole library amnesty thing blows up in our faces?*

"Jessica, you can tell my fortune after school if you want," Sarah Thomas offered as they stood in the lunch line together Thursday noon.

"Yeah, you can tell mine, too," Bruce Patman said.

"And mine, if you want," Peter DeHaven put in.

Jessica sighed dramatically. These were all kids she'd offered to tell fortunes for at Bruce's party. Where were they then? Swimming! Playing volleyball! Eating!

No, they waited until Jessica had proven herself to be a star, and now they expected her to drop everything and tell their fortunes, too. *Now I know how Johnny Buck must feel.* Johnny Buck was Jessica's favorite rock star. *When you're famous, your life just isn't your own anymore!*

Jessica waved her arms to get everyone's attention. "Listen up, everybody! Madame Jessica speaks!"

All around the cafeteria, kids shushed each other and faces turned to Jessica. She felt of rush of excitement. She had them all in the palm of her hand. "Madame Jessica will see no one else until the school fair on Saturday," she announced.

"Aw, come on! No fair!" Aaron Dallas groaned.

Jessica grinned. Making them wait was only going to add to their excitement.

Jessica paid for her ham sandwich and soup. Then she crossed the cafeteria and dropped exhaustedly into her chair at the Unicorner. "I can hardly go anywhere anymore without getting mobbed," she said, putting her hand to her forehead. She couldn't resist rubbing it in. "I knew people would be interested in my psychic ability, but I never expected *this*!"

Janet Howell rolled her eyes. "Oh, please!" she said. "You made two predictions that came true. Two lucky guesses does not make you a psychic!"

"You just haven't seen the full range of my powers," Jessica said with a shrug. "I've been able to see into the future my entire life. My parents wanted me to have a normal childhood, so I never really had the chance to go public before. But then I realized, when you've got a gift like mine, you practically have an obligation to share it with others."

"Does that mean you'll share it with your fellow Unicorns?" Lila asked. "*Before* Saturday?"

"Lila!" Janet shot Lila a warning look. "She's a fake. She can't really look into the future!"

"I don't know," Lila said. "If she can predict Patrick Morris and Sophia Rizzo breaking up, maybe she can predict who I'm going to get together with."

"Can you do that, Jessica?" Tamara asked hopefully. "Can you tell us the name of the next boy who's going to ask us out?"

"Sure." Jessica shrugged. "My powers are endless."

Lila, Ellen, Tamara, and Kimberly all turned to Jessica with hope in their eyes.

"Give me a break," Janet muttered.

Jessica loved upstaging Janet for a change. She turned to the others. "But, come on, guys," she said. "Would it be fair if I told fortunes for you when I just got through saying no more fortunes until the fair? I'm sorry, but you'll just have to wait until Saturday like everyone else."

Janet snorted. "The only reason you won't tell any fortunes before Saturday is because you know they won't come true, and then you'll be sitting in your booth all alone, wishing you'd stuck with the Unicorns!"

"We'll see who's going to be wishing they'd gone with whom on Saturday," Jessica said, leaning back in her chair with satisfaction.

Five

"Don't close the car door yet!" Jessica yelled as she dug her nails into Elizabeth's arm. "You're going to slam it on my bottom scarf if you're not careful."

Elizabeth sighed as she watched Jessica yank all her scarves out of the car. "I don't know why you had to wear all that on the way over here," she said. "Why couldn't you just change when you got here?"

"I like to make an entrance," Jessica said as she tugged her gypsy blouse into place and poufed up the sleeves.

"Have a good day, girls." Mr. Wakefield leaned through the open car window. "I'll be back to pick you up when the fair is over."

"OK. Thanks, Dad," Elizabeth said as she slammed the door closed.

Then she followed Jessica up the walk to the old Sweet Valley Fire Station #1. There was a huge banner hanging above the two oversize garage doors.

WELCOME TO THE SWEET VALLEY MIDDLE SCHOOL FAIR, it read.

Jessica groaned. "I still don't understand why we had to have the fair in an old abandoned fire station. It's going to be *dirty* in there!"

Elizabeth rolled her eyes. "It'll be fine, Jess. We were lucky to find a place that's big enough to hold all our booths. Plus, nobody else will be using it when we're not, so we can keep everything set up in between each Saturday."

"There you are!" Todd Wilkins ran outside to meet them. He was dressed in jeans, a Sweet Valley Middle School T-shirt, and an apron from Hot Dogs Are Us. "Ms. Luster's been looking all over for you, Elizabeth. She needs to go around and check on all the booths, so she was hoping you could take care of things at the library amnesty booth."

"I'd better get in there," Elizabeth said. "Can you get set up OK by yourself, Jess?"

"Sure," Jessica replied. "What's to set up? Everything I need is right here," she said, pointing to her head.

Elizabeth grinned. "Well, good luck," she said. Then she dashed inside.

"Hi, Elizabeth!" Ms. Luster said cheerfully as soon as Elizabeth walked into the building. The fair wasn't officially open yet, but there were teachers and students milling around.

The library amnesty booth was the first booth inside the door. Elizabeth entered it from behind.

"I'm so glad to see you," Ms. Luster said as Elizabeth closed the door behind her. Elizabeth had never seen Ms. Luster looking so casual. She was wearing jeans and a T-shirt, and some of her hair was falling out of a loose ponytail in back. "I need to go around and make sure we've got somebody at each booth. Can you make a sign about the free pizza for whoever returns the most overdue book? And maybe get this notebook organized so we can keep track of just how overdue the books are when they come in?"

"Sure, no problem," Elizabeth said.

Ms. Luster breathed a sigh of relief. "I can always count on you," she said, squeezing Elizabeth's hand. She grabbed a black clipboard and hurried out the door.

Elizabeth began at once to make her sign. On a large poster board she wrote FREE LARGE PIZZA FROM GUIDO'S FOR THE MOST OVERDUE LIBRARY BOOK.

That looks good, she told herself. She grabbed a staple gun and stapled her sign to the back wall of the booth.

"That sign must be some sort of trick to get people to admit just how overdue their book is," said a voice behind her.

Elizabeth turned around. "Oh, hi, Mr. Bowman!" she said cheerfully. Mr. Bowman was her English teacher and the adviser to the *Sixers*. "No. We're hoping a free pizza might motivate people to look harder for overdue library books, or maybe it'll make people feel less embarrassed about bringing back a book that's really overdue."

Mr. Bowman held up a worn copy of *A Tale of Two Cities*. "I'm afraid I'm *still* pretty embarrassed about how overdue this book is," he said sheepishly. "I've had it since the beginning of the school year."

"Well, that's OK," Elizabeth said. "That's what the library amnesty booth is all about. Getting books back that have been out a long time." She opened the notebook Ms. Luster had left on the counter. "Let's see. We should write this down. You never know. You just might win the free pizza."

"Oh, I hope not," Mr. Bowman said with a short laugh. "It wouldn't look very good if a *teacher* won the prize for most overdue book."

Elizabeth laughed as she made columns down the first sheet in the notebook. On the top line she wrote: NAME, NAME OF BOOK, DATE DUE, and DATE RETURNED. Then she slid the notebook across to Mr. Bowman. "Why don't you fill that out," she said.

Elizabeth checked the due date on the inside cover of Mr. Bowman's book, then she counted from that date to today's date, using the calendar Ms. Luster had left on the counter. "Wow, that's sixteen weeks overdue!" she announced.

"Well, I sure hope you get some other books that are more overdue than that," Mr. Bowman said with a wink.

"Jessica, don't you think five dollars is a bit much to charge?" Ms. Luster asked.

It was five past nine, and Jessica was not allowed to open her booth until this minor detail had been taken care of.

"Not really," Jessica said honestly. "Other professional psychics charge twenty five dollars."

Ms. Luster smiled. "You're not a professional psychic, Jessica. You're a sixth-grade student. And I'm sorry. I just can't allow you to charge five dollars at this booth."

Jessica sighed. "So what do you want me to charge? Two fifty?"

"I was thinking more like fifty cents."

"Fifty cents!" Jessica cried. "That's practically nothing."

"That's what all the other booths are charging."

"But—" Jessica was all set to argue, but the look on Ms. Luster's face was firm. "Oh, all right," she said. "I just hope these people realize what an incredible bargain they're getting!"

Jessica grabbed Ms. Luster's Magic Marker and went out to the front of her booth. The crowd cheered when she appeared.

Jessica could hardly believe her eyes. She had known there was a crowd out here, but she had no idea of how *big* a crowd. There was a line of customers that circled her booth three times! Jessica stood on her tiptoes and looked around. None of the other booths had a line at all.

"We want Madame Jessica! We want Madame Jessica!" the crowd chanted.

Wow! I'd better get this booth opened, Jessica told herself. She quickly crossed off the $5 on the sign outside and wrote 50¢ in its place. When she did that, the crowd really went crazy.

Jessica waved to her public and took a bow. Then she hurried back behind the curtain to her chair.

"Good luck, Jessica," Ms. Luster said.

"Thanks," Jessica replied. Then she slid the curtain open.

Her first customer was Aaron Dallas. He plunked

two quarters down on the counter and smiled at Jessica. "So what does the great and powerful Madame Jessica see for me?" he asked, leaning over the counter. He was so big he took up most of the booth.

"Let's just see," Jessica said as she took Aaron's large hands. She bowed her head in concentration. "I see a large open space," she said. "A basketball court, perhaps."

"Yeah?" Aaron said with excitement. Aaron was among the best basketball players on the team.

"I see you walking off the court . . ." Jessica went on.

"Walking or being carried on someone's shoulders?" Aaron interrupted. "They do that, you know, if you score a lot of points."

"Oh, you're definitely walking," Jessica said. "In fact, you're walking all by yourself. Nobody's very happy with you."

Jessica paused to check out Aaron's reaction.

"Go on," Aaron said, swallowing hard.

"Well," Jessica said carefully. "The coach is sort of *yelling* at you. It looks like you've been suspended."

"What!" Aaron cried. "Why am I suspended?"

Jessica shrugged. "I don't know. I don't offer explanations. I only report what I see."

"I don't believe this," Elizabeth said as she shook a copy of *Mexico, Our Neighbor to the South* at Tom McKay. "This book was due last *year*!"

Tom looked down at his feet. "I know," he said. "I didn't realize I had it until last summer when I cleaned my room."

"Well, if you found it last summer, why didn't you return it when school started this fall? We probably ordered another copy of this book because we thought it was lost." Elizabeth opened the inside cover and found the price. "That's twenty dollars we could have spent on something else if you'd only brought this back after a reasonable period of time!"

"Well, excuse me!" Tom said, glaring at her. "Man, if I'd known I was going to get hassled for returning this, I wouldn't have bothered."

Ms. Luster touched Elizabeth's shoulder. "I think what's important is that Tom *did* bring the book back," she said gently. She looked at the record book. "It looks like that's going to put you in first place for the most overdue book, Tom."

Tom's face brightened at the news. "You mean, I could win the free pizza?" he asked.

Elizabeth crossed her arms. *In Tom's case, not paying the overdue fine ought to be prize enough*, she thought. She couldn't believe he had kept a book out for an entire *year*.

"Hey, dude," Bruce Patman said as he was walking by. "What are you doing returning an overdue book *today*? You should've waited until the last week of the fair. What if someone else wins that pizza for returning a book that's only a week more overdue than yours?"

Tom slapped his forehead. "I never thought of that," he said as he and Bruce walked away.

Elizabeth frowned. "Maybe offering a prize for the most overdue book wasn't such a good idea," she said to Ms. Luster. "We don't want people to return their books just to get a chance at the prize. We want people to return them because it's the right thing to do."

"Oh, I don't know," Ms. Luster said. "If offering a free pizza is going to get kids to return their overdue books, I'm all for it. In fact, if we did that every now and then throughout the school year, we'd probably spend less on the pizza than we would on replacing all the lost library books."

"I guess," Elizabeth said. But if people would just return their books in the first place, the library wouldn't have to waste money on lost books *or* pizza. Was that really asking so much of people? To bring back a library book on time?

Six

"Are we ready to add the ice yet?" Ellen asked.

"Yes," Janet said, looking wearily at the dunk tank. Making a giant tank of Jell-O had turned out to be a lot harder than she'd thought. Just filling up the tank had taken a whole two hours—two hours during which everyone at the fair seemed to be heading toward Jessica's booth. "And let's hurry up about it so we can get this booth opened!"

Each Unicorn grabbed a bag of ice from the box. Unfortunately, after sitting out for a couple of hours, the bags had started to melt. "Oh, no," Grace said. "Do you think we've got enough ice left?"

"Let's hope so," Janet said.

While the other Unicorns tore open the ice and plunked it into the pool, Janet swished it around with the oar from her father's boat. The ice melted quickly, but the murky purple liquid never really jelled.

"It looks more like grape Kool-Aid than grape Jell-O," Ellen said.

"I can see that!" Janet said as she stared miserably into the pool. What did they do wrong?

"Maybe the water wasn't hot enough," Mandy suggested. She picked up one of the discarded bags and read the directions on the back. "It says here the water is supposed to be *boiling*."

"This water was *never* boiling," Kimberly said. "And we've had it on for more than two hours. We probably used up all the hot water."

"You mean, we've been putting in cold water?" Ellen asked.

"Great!" Janet muttered, tapping her foot. "Just great. So now what are we going to do?"

Before anybody could offer any suggestions, Coach Cassels showed up. He had promised to be their first customer. "How are we doing over here?" he asked. He looked into the tank, and his eyes widened. "What is *that*?"

"Jell-O?" Mandy offered.

"It didn't exactly turn out quite right," Mary said.

"But we're working on it," Janet assured him.

"Well, the fair's been open for two hours now," Coach said. "I don't think you ladies should waste any more time. Why don't you just go ahead and use it as it is."

The Unicorns all looked at one another. "Well, no one knows it was supposed to be Jell-O," Mandy pointed out.

"Yeah, people might think we meant to have purple water," Grace added.

Janet looked at the purple pool doubtfully.

Somehow dunking teachers in purple water just wasn't the same as dunking them in purple Jell-O.

"You know, if you don't start soon, I'll bet everyone will spend all their money getting their fortunes told." Coach Cassels gestured toward Jessica's booth with amusement. "That Jessica Wakefield is something else. Looks like she's the real star of the fair."

Janet felt her cheeks heat up. If anyone thought that Jessica's booth was more exciting than *hers*, they were nuts. "OK, Coach," she said with determination. "It's dunking time!"

"How are we doing?" Amy Sutton asked as she entered the amnesty booth through the back door. Elizabeth and Ms. Luster were sorting books at the counter.

Elizabeth glanced over her shoulder and smiled at her friend. "Not bad. You see all these books?" she asked, gesturing to the several stacks on the counter and the floor. "They've all come in today."

"Wow!" Amy's eyes widened in amazement. "Having this booth was a great idea, Ms. Luster."

"I'm glad you think so," Ms. Luster replied. "Elizabeth has been having second thoughts."

Amy turned to Elizabeth. "Really? How come?"

"Well, just think how much money we would've earned in fines if all the people who returned those books had paid up," Elizabeth said. "That money could have gone to buy new books."

"I don't know," Amy said. "If we were collecting fines today, I don't think we would've gotten all those books back."

"That's what I told Elizabeth," Ms. Luster said. "When people have books that are extremely over-due, they'll usually just keep the books and stop using the library."

"But that's not right." Elizabeth shook her head. "When you check out a library book, you have a moral obligation to return it on time. I think we need to think of ways to get people to live up to their responsibilities."

While they were talking, Charlie Cashman came up to them with a copy of *Sports Car* magazine. "Can we return overdue magazines here, too?" he asked.

Ms. Luster nodded as she took the magazine from Charlie. "Any overdue library materials can be returned here."

"Great! I checked this out a couple of *years* ago. It must be one of the most overdue things you've gotten, huh?" Charlie asked with pride.

Ms. Luster ran her finger down the list of due dates in the record book. "I think you're right, Charlie," she said. "So far the prize for most overdue item belongs to you."

"All right!" Charlie cried.

Elizabeth sighed. This whole library amnesty project was becoming a joke. People weren't even sorry about keeping their books out so long. All they cared about was whether or not they had a shot at winning the free pizza.

"Don't go ordering that pizza just yet." A tall man with a dark beard came up behind Charlie. "It's going to be hard for anyone to top this one," he said. He held up a worn paperback copy of the *1978 Guinness Book of World Records*. "This was practically brand-new when I checked it out."

Elizabeth's mouth dropped open. "You mean, you checked that out in 1978?" she asked incredulously.

"In 1979, actually," the man replied. "I missed a lot of school in those last couple of months, so it never got returned. And then the next year, I went on to high school, and well, you know . . ." He ran his hand through his hair. He looked really embarrassed.

Ms. Luster took the book from the man. "I'm afraid a 1979 book of records isn't as much in demand today as it was back then," she said. "But I thank you for returning it nonetheless."

The man filled in the information about the record book, then left.

Charlie drummed his fingers on the counter as he watched the guy walk away. "That guy can't win the pizza, can he?" he asked in a worried voice. "I mean, he's not even a student at Sweet Valley Middle School."

"He can win," Ms. Luster said. "The prize goes to the most overdue item. No matter who turns it in."

"But that's not fair," Charlie argued. "We don't have a chance against all those old people who might have old library books lying around."

"Isn't it enough that you got to return your magazine without paying a fine?" Elizabeth asked.

Ms. Luster touched Elizabeth's arm. "You've been working hard all morning, Elizabeth," she said gently. "I think maybe it's time you took a break."

Elizabeth looked at Ms. Luster. Was this her way of telling Elizabeth to ease up a little?

Elizabeth glanced down at her feet. Maybe she *was* going a little overboard. But it bothered her to see people taking such advantage of the library amnesty project.

"Maybe I do need a break," Elizabeth said after a while. Maybe if she got away for a while, she'd come back feeling refreshed and ready to deal with all the overdue books, no matter *how* overdue they were.

"Just mustard. No ketchup. Right?" Todd Wilkins asked from behind the counter of the food booth.

Elizabeth smiled. "That's right," she said. She loved that Todd knew exactly how she liked her hot dogs. A lot of boys wouldn't pay such close attention. Maybe a little food was just what she needed to get her mind off the library amnesty project.

"Hey, you guys," Patrick Morris said, stepping up to the counter. He was wearing his saxophone around his neck. "Can I get a bag of chips and a coke?" He set his money on the counter.

"Sure," Todd said.

"Do we get a concert?" Elizabeth asked, gesturing to Patrick's saxophone.

"Sure." Patrick smiled. "The whole band's playing in about twenty minutes."

"Great," Todd said as he set the drink and chips down on the counter.

Patrick sat down on the stool beside Elizabeth. He opened his bag of chips, but he didn't take any. He just sat with his shoulders hunched and stirred the ice in his drink. "Have either of you seen Sophia?" he asked after a couple of minutes. "Do you know if she's here today?"

"You two didn't come together?" Elizabeth asked.

Patrick shook his head sadly. "Thanks to your sister, she's not talking to me. Remember?"

Elizabeth frowned. She had forgotten about that. "Come on, Patrick," she said. "You're the one who forgot her birthday. Jessica had nothing to do with that."

Patrick sighed. "I know, Elizabeth. I'm sorry. I just miss her."

Elizabeth touched Patrick's arm. "You guys will work it out," she said.

"I don't know," Patrick said as he stared at his feet.

Elizabeth could tell he wasn't holding out much hope.

"I'll see you guys later," he said as he got up.

Elizabeth looked after him. "Poor Patrick," she said once he was gone.

"Yeah," Todd agreed. "He's in bad shape. Say, have you seen your sister in action today?"

"Not yet," Elizabeth said.

"I heard she's been predicting nothing but doom and gloom all morning," Todd told her. "But people have been lining up over there like crazy. She's really raking in cash for the library."

Elizabeth turned. She could see a line from Jessica's booth all the way to one of the big firehouse doors. It was incredible. "Maybe I should take her a hot dog and drink," Elizabeth said. "She might not get a chance to eat if I don't."

"I feel pain," Elizabeth heard Jessica say as she tiptoed in through the back of Madame Jessica's booth.

Bruce Patman was standing at her window. "What sort of pain?" he asked skeptically.

"Pain in my ankle," she replied. "I'm sorry to have to tell you this, Bruce, but I think you're going to sprain your ankle."

"Yeah, right," Bruce snorted. "Like you can really predict something like that."

"Madame Jessica knows all," Jessica said. She sounded so confident, that for a minute, Elizabeth actually believed Bruce would sprain his ankle.

"Who's next?" Jessica asked.

Sarah Thomas stepped forward. Elizabeth stood quietly in the back corner and listened.

"I feel pain for you, too, Sarah," Jessica said. "But with you it's not in my ankle, it's in my mouth. I think you're going to get your braces tightened."

Sarah groaned. "Not again," she moaned.

Todd wasn't kidding, Elizabeth thought. *Jessica was predicting a lot of bad things.* She wondered how long such a negative fortune-teller would remain popular.

Just then Jessica whirled around. "I thought I heard . . . er, felt your presence. What are you doing here?" she asked.

"I thought you might be hungry, so I brought you some lunch," she said, holding up the hot dog and drink.

"Oh, you're a lifesaver!" Jessica said, grabbing the drink. "I am *so* thirsty!" She drank almost half the cup in one long swallow. When she finished, she leaned out her booth and cupped her hands around her mouth. "Listen up, everybody!" she shouted. "Madame Jessica is going to tell one more fortune and then she's going to take a lunch break."

Everyone groaned.

"I'm sorry, but Madame Jessica needs nourishment

just like anybody else," she said. "OK. Who's next?"

Anna Reynolds stepped forward while all the other kids slowly drifted away.

"That's a great jacket," Jessica said, gesturing toward Anna's black leather jacket. Elizabeth thought it was gorgeous too.

"Thanks," Anna replied. "My mom just bought it for me." Anna was deaf, so when she talked, her words sounded a little fuzzier than everybody else's. But you could understand her. And she could understand other people because she could read lips.

Jessica scrunched her face up in concentration. "Oh, no," she said. "I see you without this jacket. I think you're going to lose it somehow."

"Oh!" Looking stricken, Anna abruptly stood up and walked away from the booth.

Jessica reached under the counter and pulled out a sign with a clock on it that said, "Back at . . ." She spun the hands to read 1:00, propped it up on her counter, and closed the curtain. "Wow," she said as she spun around on her chair. "This has been the most incredible morning!"

"So I see," Elizabeth said. "But tell me, Jess. Why is it that every single one of your fortunes is bad?"

Jessica looked a little insulted. "Elizabeth," she said. "The future is not always bright." Then she picked up her hot dog and began eating eagerly.

Seven

"You call that Jell-O?" Jessica asked as she stared into the purple dunking tank. The fair had closed for the day and Jessica had wandered back to the Unicorn booth to see how they had done.

"Well, the Jell-O didn't exactly turn out quite right," Lila admitted.

Jessica peered into the pool. It was kind of a murky, purple mess. "I guess not," she said. Then she burst out laughing.

"Give us a break, Jessica," Mary said softly. "Have you ever tried to mix five hundred gallons of Jell-O at one time?"

"No." Jessica shook her head. "But I could've told you it wouldn't work." She put her fingers to her temples. "Madame Jessica sees all."

"Oh, stop with the Madame Jessica stuff already!" Janet blurted out. "I'm tired of it. So we had a little setback with the Jell-O. We've still got the best booth here!"

"Oh, really?" Jessica smiled. "Well, I couldn't really see past the lines at my booth to see how you guys were doing," she said breezily. "But I made over thirty-eight dollars today. How much did you guys make?"

"Thirty-eight dollars!" Ellen's eyebrows shot up. "Wow. We barely made two."

Janet glared at Ellen. "That's because we opened so late," she said through clenched teeth.

"I don't think anybody else made as much money as I did," Jessica continued. "They might have to change the name of the library from the Sweet Valley Middle School Library to the *Jessica Wakefield* Library."

"Well, we've got the kinks worked out of our system now," Janet said as she stood face to face with Jessica. "Just wait until next week, when all of your fortunes have turned out to be a bust. We'll see whose booth everybody will be lining up at then!"

Jessica crossed her arms. "Yes, we will, won't we," she said confidently.

"I couldn't believe how overdue some of the books we got back were," Elizabeth said at dinner that night. "There was this one guy who returned a book from 1979. I thought he was going to win the most-overdue-book prize for sure. But then some eighth-grader's dad brought back a book he had checked out in 1972! Can you believe it? That's more than twenty years overdue!"

"Twenty years?" Jessica cried, her mouth full of mashed potatos. "We weren't even born when that book was checked out!"

"Yeah, isn't that incredible?" Elizabeth asked.

"What's incredible is that the guy still had the book after all those years," Mr. Wakefield said as he cut his meat.

"It just goes to show you what a good project you've got going here, Elizabeth," Mrs. Wakefield said. "You're getting back books that you probably never would have otherwise."

"Well, I'm just amazed at how many irresponsible library users we have," Elizabeth said.

"Oh, like you've never had an overdue library book," Steven said.

"I've had an overdue library book," Elizabeth replied. "But never more than just a few days overdue. And I've always paid the fine."

"Well, bully for you," Steven said.

Elizabeth stuck out her tongue at her brother.

"I predict you'll get an even more overdue book than that one that was due in 1972," Jessica said.

"Oh, well if *Madame Jessica* predicts it, it's bound to happen," Steven said sarcastically.

"Steven," Mrs. Wakefield said in a warning voice. Then she turned back to Elizabeth. "It could happen. There are still two weeks left of the fair."

"A lot can happen in two weeks," Mr. Wakefield added as he poured himself another glass of water. "How was your booth, Jessica?"

Jessica smiled. "It was terrific," she said. "I think I earned more money for the library than anybody else. I had to actually kick people out just so I could have some lunch. That was the only break I got all day."

"Oh, poor baby," Steven said, giving her a phony

sympathetic look. "It's so rough being psychic."

"Jessica's booth was probably the most popular booth at the whole fair," Elizabeth said loyally. "Every time I looked over there, she had a line."

"I can't believe people would stand in line just to hear you make up some stupid fortune that won't come true," Steven said.

"My fortunes always come true," Jessica said. "Don't they, Lizzie?"

"Well . . ." Elizabeth didn't know quite how to answer that. She *hoped* they wouldn't all come true.

"I could tell your fortune, too, if you want, Steven," Jessica offered.

"No thanks," Steven said. "I heard what kind of fortunes you tell."

Jessica gave him a knowing look. "I thought you didn't believe my fortunes came true."

"I don't," Steven said. "But I wouldn't want you to feel guilty if you predicted a brick would fall on my head and one actually did."

"Why should I feel guilty?" Jessica shrugged. "I'm not responsible for what I see when I look into the future."

Sophia's heart started pounding when she saw Patrick coming down the hall Monday morning. She hadn't spoken to Patrick for exactly seven days. It seemed like forever.

"Hey, Sophia!" Patrick called. Sophia could barely see him through kids crowding the hallway.

Sophia felt a burst of hope. Maybe he'd brought her flowers or something to apologize for forgetting

her birthday. Wasn't that what guys did after they'd
been jerks? Brought flowers?

But when Patrick finally made it over to her, all
she saw was his smiling face. The only thing he was
carrying was his math book. "Have you forgiven me
yet?" he asked as he cocked his head in that cute
puppy-dog look he had.

Sophia narrowed her eyes. Did he really think
that stupid look was going to work on her when
he knew how upset she was? She clucked her
tongue and turned away from him without an-
swering.

"Come on, Sophia," he said. He took her hand
as he shuffled along beside her. "I said I was
sorry."

"And that's it?" She whipped her head around to
face him. "You're sorry?"

"Um—sure," he said uncertainly. "What—uh—
more do you want?"

Sophia pulled her hand away. "Nothing," she said.
She shouldn't have to tell him. He should be able to
figure it out for himself.

"You don't really want to break up, do you?" he
asked.

Sophia felt her face heat up. Of course she didn't
want to break up. She just wanted her so-called boyfriend to show a little consideration.

"I mean, we don't have to break up just because
Jessica said we would," Patrick said.

Sophia stopped walking. "Who said we're going
to break up because of Jessica?"

Patrick smiled. "So you *do* forgive me?"

Sophia shook her head.

Patrick's face fell. "So what are you saying?"

Sophia sighed. She'd never realized Patrick was so dense. "You figure it out," she said.

"Oh, my gosh!" Jessica exclaimed when she saw Bruce Patman hobbling into science class just after the bell rang. He was on crutches. His right leg was bandaged from his toes to his knee.

"You really did sprain your ankle!"

"Actually I tore a few ligaments," he grumbled.

"Close enough!" Jessica squealed with glee. She glanced around the room. Were all these kids aware that she, the Incredible Madame Jessica, had predicted this terrible tragedy?

"How did it happen?" Peter Burns asked.

"Playing baseball yesterday," Bruce replied. He used his hand to demonstrate. "I was sliding into home, when all of a sudden, POW!" he slapped his hand. "My cousin piled his gigantuan body on top of me."

Jessica smiled triumphantly. "I told you this would happen."

Peter turned to look at her.

"I did," Jessica insisted. "At the fair on Saturday. And you didn't believe me, Bruce. That just goes to show you. You should never underestimate the power of a true psychic."

Bruce snorted. "You probably *made* it happen."

"Oh, right," Jessica said, rolling her eyes. "I took over your cousin's gigantuan body and pounced on you myself, spraining your ankle."

"Tearing my ligaments," Bruce corrected.

"Whatever." Jessica waved her hand dismissively.

"You might as well give it up, Bruce, and accept the obvious fact that I'm psychic."

Mr. Seigel came into the room then and closed the door. "OK, people," he said, rapping his pointing stick against his table. "The bell has rung, so let's settle down. We've got some important material to cover today."

Oh yeah, Jessica thought. *Real important!* They were talking about the life cycle of a cell. When would they ever need to know *that* in real life?

Jessica immediately waved her hand in the air. "Mr. Seigel? I've got something even more important than cells to talk about."

Mr. Seigel crossed his arms. "And what could that be, Jessica?" he asked, glancing at his watch.

"I think we should discuss the psychic phenomenon," she said importantly.

"I'm afraid the psychic phenomenon doesn't have much to do with physical science," Mr. Seigel said.

"Sure it does," Jessica argued. "Science is about proving stuff, right? Well, I can prove I'm psychic. Just look at Bruce's leg. No regular person could've predicted that."

"Jessica, if you really are psychic, you should already know that this discussion is over," Mr. Seigel said. "But for the rest of you who were not blessed with Jessica's unique vision, let's turn to page one seventy-eight in our texts."

Jessica sighed. Mr. Seigel had no clue about what really mattered in life.

"What's wrong, Anna?" Elizabeth asked. She was just getting ready to leave her English class when she noticed Anna was frantically turning around in her seat, looking for something.

"You don't have her attention," Cammie Adams said. Cammie knew about communicating with the hearing-impaired because both her parents were deaf. She leaned across the aisle and touched Anna's arm.

Anna glanced up at Cammie, and Cammie pointed to Elizabeth.

"What's the matter?" Elizabeth asked again.

"My jacket," Anna explained. "It's not here."

Elizabeth thought back to Saturday, when Anna was wearing that gorgeous new jacket. Jessica had told Anna that she would lose it. But Elizabeth quickly pushed that thought away. It was just a coincidence. "Are you sure you had it when you walked in here forty five minutes ago?" she asked.

Anna had already turned away, so she had no idea what Elizabeth had asked. She was down on her hands and knees, searching under the nearby chairs.

Cammie touched Anna's arm again. She signed something to her. Anna signed something back.

"What's she saying?" Elizabeth asked.

"She said she thought she had it, but maybe she didn't."

"What class did you have before this one?" Elizabeth asked.

"Gym," Anna replied.

"Well, maybe you left it in the locker room," Elizabeth said. "Why don't we go down there and see?"

"Hey, what's going on?" Jessica asked as she stopped at Elizabeth's desk.

"Anna can't find her jacket," Elizabeth replied.

"She can't?" Jessica squealed with delight.

Elizabeth nudged her sister, and Jessica quickly wiped the smile off her face. "I mean, that's terrible," Jessica said. "But you know, I did tell her this would happen."

Elizabeth glared at Jessica. "We were just going to go down to the girls' locker room and see if she left it there."

"She didn't," Jessica said confidently. "I'm sure of it."

"I want to look," Anna said as her eyes began to fill with tears.

"It's not here," Anna said sadly once they'd made their way to her locker.

"Maybe it's inside your locker," Elizabeth suggested.

"I don't think a jacket would fit in these tiny gym lockers," Jessica said as if it would be pointless to even look.

But Anna spun the combination on her lock anyway. She pulled her locker open. Her face fell. All that was inside was her gym clothes.

"You can come back later and ask Ms. Langberg if she picked it up," Cammie said softly as she put an arm around Anna.

Anna nodded, biting her lip.

"That won't do any good." Jessica shook her head. "Face it, guys. Anna's jacket is gone. Gone for good!"

"Jessica!" Elizabeth shot her sister a warning look. She really could not believe Jessica's nerve.

"I'm sorry," Jessica said, holding out her hands helplessly. "But I see no reason to pretend it's going to show up when it's not. I *told* her this would happen."

"Is that all that matters to you?" Elizabeth asked with a hand on her hip. "The fact that one of your predictions has come true?"

"Well, it's not just *one* prediction, Lizzie." Jessica gave a short laugh. Her eyes glowed with excitement. "It's *all* of my predictions. They're all coming true. I mean, don't I just blow you all away?"

"Yes, you sure do," Elizabeth said quietly.

Jessica opened her front door and picked up the newspaper. Her face was on the front page. The headline read "Former Sweet Valley native claims Nobel Peace Prize."

Suddenly there were about twenty cameras in her face. Jessica had to shade her eyes from all the bright lights.

"Tell me, Ms. Wakefield, how were you able to tell the FBI the exact location of the bomb before it went off?" one reporter asked.

Before Jessica could answer, another reporter stepped forward. "Were you aware this bomb had the capacity to destroy Los Angeles and every other city within a two-hundred-mile radius?"

"The entire United States is in your debt," a third reporter interrupted. "Because of your incredible psychic power, we were able to discover the bomb and detonate it before it could cause any damage. How does that make you feel?"

"Well." Jessica shrugged modestly. "I've always wanted to use my gift for good."

"And it is truly a gift." A handsome male reporter stepped forward. "Tell me, Ms. Wakefield—"

"Please, call me Jessica," Jessica said.

The reporter smiled. "Jessica, tell me, when was it you discovered this marvelous gift?"

"I'm not sure," Jessica replied thoughtfully. "I've al-ways been psychic, but it was really during the Sweet Valley Middle School Fair that I went public with it."

"The Sweet Valley Middle School Fair," he said as though he remembered it fondly. "Why, that was where we discovered you."

The roar of applause filled Jessica's ears.

Applause?

Or was it thunder?

Jessica bolted up in bed. It *was* thunder. And the whole thing had been just a dream.

But sometimes dreams become reality, Jessica thought with a glimmer of excitement. After all, almost every one of her predictions had come true. At least partly. And it was only Tuesday.

Jessica pulled the covers up to her chin and shiv-ered. "I am so incredibly psychic, I scare myself," she whispered into the darkness.

Eight

◇

Janet nearly jumped out of her skin as Aaron Dallas slammed his locker door. He slammed it so hard that the metal door didn't even latch. It swung open and banged against the next locker over. Aaron slammed it again.

"Hey, what's your problem?" Janet asked in an annoyed voice. It was Wednesday morning, and Janet was sitting on a heating duct across from the lockers, trying to study for her algebra test. Sheets of rain pounded the window behind her.

"I'm temporarily suspended from the basketball team," Aaron griped.

Janet stared at him with disbelief. Aaron was only a sixth-grader, but he was one of the best players on the team. How could he have been suspended? "What happened?" she asked.

Aaron let out a miserable sigh. "Coach says I dropped below a C average. So until my grades improve, I'm off the team."

"That's too bad," Janet said as she thought of all the games Sweet Valley would be losing without Aaron on the team.

Aaron leaned against a locker. "I should've listened to Jessica," he said, shaking his head sadly.

Janet had been hearing Jessica's name so much lately, she was ready to scream.

"She told me this would happen, but I didn't believe her," Aaron went on. "In fact, I was kind of mad at her."

"Really?" Janet leaned a little closer. She knew that Aaron and Jessica were sort of going together.

"Well, yeah," Aaron said with a puzzled look. "I mean, I figured Jessica would give her friends good fortunes. I had no idea this psychic stuff was for real. I should've taken her seriously," he said, shaking his head.

Oh please! Janet thought. *Take Jessica Wakefield seriously?*

"Did you know that just about everything Jessica predicted has come true?" Aaron asked. "People can hardly wait until Saturday to have their fortunes told again."

"I can't imagine why," Janet grumbled. "I heard that practically all her fortunes were bad ones."

"Yeah, but no one really cares about that," Aaron said. "Everyone's just so amazed that she's *right* all the time!"

Janet snorted. "Well, I certainly wouldn't want her to tell *my* fortune. It's like having a bad curse put on you!"

Aaron's eyes widened to the size of golf balls. "Do you really think she has that kind of power?"

Janet smiled. She hadn't expected Aaron to take her seriously. But since he did . . . well, she might as well use it to her advantage.

"You have to admit, a lot of bad things have been happening around here since Jessica opened her fortune-telling booth," Janet said mysteriously.

"Yeah, they have," Aaron said nervously.

"You wouldn't catch me within ten feet of Jessica Wakefield," Janet said.

Aaron chewed his lip thoughtfully. "I gotta go talk to some people," he said. "I'll see you later."

"Yeah, see ya," Janet said as she watched Aaron go over to talk to Bruce Patman. Bruce leaned on his crutches and listened to whatever Aaron had to say. He looked extremely interested.

Janet smiled. "I predict you're going to be out of business by Saturday, Madame Jessica," she muttered.

Jessica hurried down the hall, determined to catch Olivia Davidson between second and third period. Olivia was one of the best artists at Sweet Valley Middle School. She and Sarah Thomas were running a design-your-own T-shirt booth at the school fair. Jessica was hoping Olivia would design a shirt for her, something she could wear around school to advertise her services.

It would definitely have to be purple, Jessica decided. And it should have a picture of her gazing thoughtfully into a crystal ball. She was trying to decide whether it would be overkill to also have about fifty adoring fans on the shirt when suddenly she plowed into some girl and knocked the books out of her hands.

"Oh! I'm so sorry," Jessica said as she bent down to help the girl retrieve her books.

"No, I should've been watching where I was going," the girl said as she pushed her glasses up onto her nose. Her face was almost as red as her hair. Jessica didn't know her personally, but she could tell by the books on the floor that she was a seventh-grader.

The girl peered curiously into Jessica's face. "Hey, you're that girl who tells the fortunes, aren't you?" she said as she stood up.

"That's right." Jessica straightened her shoulders, pleased to see she was becoming so famous. "Would you like me to tell your fortune?"

The girl shook her head quickly. "No thanks," she said, shifting her books.

"Oh, come on," Jessica insisted as she handed the girl one of her books. "I'll do it for free. It's only fair after I knocked your books on the floor."

But the girl shook her head even harder. "No. Please don't," she said. Then she took off up the stairs.

Whatever. Jessica shrugged. As she continued down the hall, she spotted Olivia coming out of her classroom.

"Hey, Olivia," Jessica yelled as she ran to catch up with her.

Olivia's brown curls danced on her shoulders as she turned. She looked right at Jessica, gasped, then dashed inside another classroom.

That was weird, Jessica thought. She was sure Olivia saw her. But before she could think anything more about it, she noticed Sarah Thomas standing in front of an open locker.

Well, maybe Sarah will make the shirt for me, Jessica thought. She ran up to Sarah and tapped her on the shoulder.

"Aaah!" Sarah jumped.

"Sorry." Jessica giggled. "Listen, I was wondering, could you make me a really cool shirt that has a picture of me on the front looking into a crystal ball?"

Sarah's eyes grew large. She took a couple steps back. "Uh, well, I don't know," she stammered.

"I could pay you your going rate, or if you'd rather, I could pay you in services," Jessica offered, her eyes sparkling. "You know, give you a certificate for free fortune-telling for a month or something like that."

"No!" Sarah cried. "I mean, I don't think we can do something that elaborate." She took a few steps back. "Listen, I have to get to class. So bye!"

"Bye," Jessica replied, even though Sarah was already running down the hall.

"Psst!"

Elizabeth glanced up. She was shelving books in the library when she heard a funny noise on the other side of the shelf.

"Psst!" *There it went again!*

Elizabeth slid some books to the side and saw Jerry McAllister peering at her through the shelves. "I need a book about somebody who's made a difference in our world in the last hundred years," he said.

"The computer catalog is right over there." Elizabeth pointed. "Just type in the name of the person you want."

Jerry smiled sheepishly. "I don't know who I

want," he said. "That's the problem. Can't you just quickly find me a book? I can't think of anybody who's made a difference in the last hundred years."

Elizabeth laughed. "Jerry, there have been more changes in the last hundred years than any other period in history. We've got computers, TV—"

"TV?" Jerry said. "You think I could do a report on the guy who invented TV?"

Elizabeth shrugged. "I don't know why not." She led Jerry to the computer catalog and showed him how to do a search. "OK, here we are. *The History of Television*. That'll be over in the seven ninety-ones."

She led Jerry over to the proper section, and together they scanned the shelves. "Here it is," she said as she pulled *The History of Television* off the shelf and handed it to Jerry.

"Cool," Jerry said. "I'll go check it out."

"You mean you're going to take it out of the library?" Elizabeth asked.

Jerry laughed. "Well, yeah. That's what I came here for."

Elizabeth felt a flicker of alarm. She remembered how she'd caught him slipping in an overdue book a couple of weeks ago. What if this time he didn't even bother returning the book at all?

But she didn't have much choice. Mrs. Arnette had sent Jerry to the library to check out a book. Elizabeth couldn't very well send him back to class without one. "Just make sure you return it when it's due," she said finally.

"Duh!" Jerry said.

"Well, you may not realize it, but when kids don't

return their library books, it hurts everybody. That's fewer books the library can order—"

"Yeah, yeah," Jerry said impatiently. "I said I'd return it. Give me a break, would you?"

Elizabeth watched as Jerry took his book up to Ms. Luster. He turned once and glared at her, then he set his book on the counter.

Elizabeth sighed. She knew she wasn't exactly making herself popular, but she couldn't help it. Ever since she'd gotten involved in the library amnesty project, she'd been feeling very protective of the library and the books inside it. Somebody had to care about the library, she decided. Most of the other kids barely gave it a second thought.

As Jessica carried her lunch tray across the cafeteria, she had the distinct feeling people were watching her. *Well, of course people are watching,* she told herself. *People always watch when a celebrity walks by.*

Then she glanced over at the Unicorner. *No one* was there.

That's weird, Jessica thought. *Where is everybody?*

She turned to see if they were back in the lunch line. But there were just a few seventh graders in line. And none of them were Unicorns.

Did they decide to eat lunch somewhere else and not tell me? Jessica wondered. *Why would they do that?*

Jessica didn't like this one bit. The star of the Sweet Valley Middle School Fair couldn't be seen eating lunch alone!

She glanced desperately around the cafeteria for someone to eat with. She saw Elizabeth across the cafeteria. But Elizabeth was eating with some of her boring friends—Amy Sutton, Maria Slater, Cammie Adams, Lloyd Benson, and Winston Egbert.

Jessica sighed. *Well, eating with the nerds of Sweet Valley is probably better than eating alone.* At least this way, people might think she was doing charity work or something. She crossed the cafeteria and set her tray down. "Hi, guys," she said cheerfully.

Suddenly everybody except Elizabeth stood up.

"Don't talk to me, Jessica," Lloyd said, shaking a finger at her. "Don't say a word!"

"Yeah, we don't want to know our futures." Winston's voice cracked.

"See you later, Elizabeth," Amy said with a sympathetic glance.

"Gotta run," Maria added.

Jessica stared dumbfounded as the six of them walked away. "What's with them?" she asked, sitting down.

"I think they were afraid you were going to tell their fortunes," Elizabeth said.

Afraid *I'd tell their fortunes?* Jessica thought incredulously. *They should be so lucky.* Then it hit her. Nerds were notoriously honest. "They didn't want me to give *free* fortunes. They wanted to wait until Saturday, so they can pay me and the money can go into the library fund."

"No." Elizabeth shook her head slowly. "I don't think that's it." She looked at her sister steadily. "I'm not sure how to break this to you, Jessica, but I don't think people are all that excited about your fortunes anymore."

"What do you mean?" Jessica wrinkled her forehead in confusion.

"Well," Elizabeth said carefully. "You always predict such horrible things, and then when they actually happen, you act all happy about it."

Jessica started to open her mouth, but she found herself at a loss for words. She *was* happy her fortunes were coming true. It proved she was really psychic. But she wasn't happy that people were having terrible things happen to them. She really wasn't.

Elizabeth touched Jessica's hand. "I'm sorry, Jess. I don't mean to hurt your feelings. But I think you should know what kids are saying."

"You didn't hurt my feelings, Lizzie," Jessica said, squaring her shoulders. "Some people have a hard time dealing with bad things. Is that my problem?"

Elizabeth gazed at her sister thoughtfully. "It is if nobody wants to have anything to do with you."

"Hey, Aaron! Wait up!" Jessica called down the hallway. She knew he was going to English class, just like she was. Maybe they could walk together.

But Aaron glanced over his shoulder at Jessica and then started walking faster.

This is unbelievable, Jessica thought. *Everyone is avoiding me!*

"What's the matter, Jessica?" Janet came up from behind her, along with Tamara. "Are you finding it a little lonely at the top?"

Tamara giggled as she and Janet hurried past.

Jessica felt tears spring into her eyes. It was great that people were taking her fortune-telling so seriously. That they believed in her power. But she couldn't have people avoiding her.

I've got to do something, she thought desperately as

she blinked the tears away. *Something that will show people they don't have to be afraid.*

The question was—what?

"I've decided to change my strategy," Jessica announced as she enterred Elizabeth's bedroom through the adjoining bathroom.

Elizabeth glanced up from her homework. "Oh?" she said curiously. "What strategy?"

"My fortune-telling strategy!" Jessica said impatiently. "From now on, I'm only going to tell good fortunes. What do you think?"

Elizabeth shrugged. "Sounds good to me."

Jessica sat down on Elizabeth's bed. "Do you think people will forget about the negative Madame Jessica if she's replaced by a more positive Madame Jessica?" she asked worriedly.

"Probably," Elizabeth guessed.

Jessica sighed with relief. "Good! Come over here and let me try it with you," she said, patting the space beside her.

Elizabeth shook her head. "I can't, Jessica. I have a ton of math to do tonight. I really want to get it done before dinner."

"Oh, come on, Lizzie. It won't take very long. Or do you think I can't tell good fortunes?" Jessica asked in a pouty voice. "Is that it? Are you afraid to let me tell your fortune?"

Elizabeth sighed. "Oh, all right." She dragged herself over to the bed. "You can tell my fortune. But make it quick."

"I will!" Jessica promised. She took her sister's hands, closed her eyes and concentrated. *Good thoughts. Nothing but good thoughts,* she told herself.

She breathed in and breathed out. "OK, I've got it!" she said with excitement. "You're going to find something. Something of value. Something that's been lost for a long time." She opened her eyes and looked at her sister. "How's that for a good fortune?"

"Fine," Elizabeth said. "Now, can I get back to my homework, please?"

"Sure, sure, go ahead." Jessica waved her away. She went back to her own room in high spirits. She'd tell a few of these good fortunes at school tomorrow so people would know that the negative Madame Jessica was gone. Her reputation would be saved. And then, come Saturday, her booth would still be the most popular booth at the school fair.

Nine

"That's funny," Elizabeth muttered in her bedroom after dinner. She was sure she'd left her math homework, which she'd meant to check over, on her dresser. But the paper was nowhere in sight.

She dropped to her knees and checked under her bed and under her dresser. There was a paper behind her dresser, but she couldn't quite reach it. She was going to have to move the dresser.

She stood up and pushed against the dresser as hard as she could. It didn't budge. She turned around and pushed with her back. It still didn't budge.

She went down the hall to Steven's room. He was lying on his bed listening to his Walkman and reading a magazine.

"Will you help me move my dresser?" Elizabeth asked.

Steven removed his headphones. "Huh?"

"Will you help me move my dresser?" Elizabeth

repeated. "I think my math paper fell down behind it, and I can't get it out."

Steven sighed loudly as he dragged himself to a sitting position. "What'll you give me if I do it?"

Elizabeth sighed. "How about the satisfaction of having helped your sister in her time of need," she replied.

"That's it?" Steven said with disappointment.

Elizabeth glared at him.

"Oh, all right," Steven moaned. "I'm coming."

He followed Elizabeth to her room. He put his hands around the dresser and gave it a firm tug. The dresser came away from the wall.

Elizabeth reached for the paper. It *was* her math paper. "Thanks, Steven!" She sighed with relief.

"Wait a minute," Steven said before he pushed the dresser back. "There's something else back there."

Elizabeth looked. There was a book on the floor. She reached down to pick it up. *Hmm.* Black Beauty? *Where did that come from?* she wondered, blowing dust off of it.

"Can I move this thing back now?" Steven asked.

Elizabeth nodded. "Please do," she said.

Steven grabbed the dresser with both hands and shoved it back into place. "There you are," he said.

"Thanks," Elizabeth replied as he left the room.

Once he was gone, Elizabeth closed her door tightly. Then she looked at the book in her hands. The cover was stamped "Sweet Valley Elementary School." *That's strange*, Elizabeth thought.

She opened the back cover and gasped. The book had been due almost four years ago!

*   *   *

Elizabeth was in a courtroom. She was filthy. Her hair hung in limp tangles down her back. She wore a dirty old brown dress.

"What is this girl's crime?" the judge asked.

Mr. Wakefield stepped forward. "She kept a library book for four years, Your Honor, but she's ready to face her punishment, whatever it may be."

"Hang her! Hang her! Hang her!" the crowd chanted.

Elizabeth bolted up in bed. Sweat poured down her face. She turned on her bedside lamp. *Black Beauty* was sitting on her night table.

Elizabeth picked up the book and stared at the cover. How could she have kept a library book for four years? How could it have sat behind her dresser all this time?

And she'd been so judgmental toward everybody else who returned an overdue library book. What would the kids at school say when they found out about *her* overdue book? What would Ms. Luster say? Some example Elizabeth had set!

Elizabeth fell back against her pillow. How could she ever live this down? She pulled the covers up over her head.

Then suddenly she flung the covers off. An idea flashed through her mind.

What if she returned the book without anybody knowing? She could return it to the library amnesty booth on Saturday and slip it into the pile sometime when Ms. Luster was on a break.

Elizabeth shivered. *What's happening to me?* she thought. *It's like I'm becoming a hardened criminal or something.*

But now that she knew she had kept a library book

out for four whole years, it seemed as if she were capable of just about anything.

"Eek!" Sarah Thomas exclaimed on Friday morning the moment she saw Jessica. She grabbed Olivia Davidson's arm and began pulling her down the hall.

Jessica hurried to catch up with them. She was wearing her psychic's costume. "Don't be afraid!" she exclaimed triumphantly. "It's a new day, and Madame Jessica predicts a bright future for all!" She waved the end of her scarf in the air with a flourish.

Sarah and Olivia exchanged doubtful looks.

"It's true," Jessica said. "The old Madame Jessica with her horrible predictions is long gone. I am the new Madame Jessica. I see only good."

Sarah and Olivia walked more quickly down the hall.

"I'll be available for consultation during lunch," Jessica called after them. "Stop and see me!"

At lunchtime Jessica went right to the center of the cafeteria and clapped her hands to get everyone's attention. "Listen up, everyone!" she said as she cupped her hands around her mouth. "Madame Jessica is making a special appearance in the cafeteria today."

The lunch line slowly inched forward. Heads were bent in conversation. No one was paying any attention to Jessica.

Jessica cleared her throat nervously. "You may have already heard the news. Madame Jessica only tells good fortunes now."

Janet Howell rolled her eyes and turned to say something to Kimberly Haver.

Jessica sighed. If only *one* person would step forward. She glanced around the cafeteria. Patrick Morris was just coming off the lunch line and was looking for a place to sit.

"Patrick!" Jessica called to him excitedly. "Would you like me to tell your fortune?"

Patrick stiffened. "No way, Jessica. You already got me in trouble with Sophia. I don't want to hear any more of your fortunes."

"But this'll be a *good* fortune," Jessica insisted. "I promise!"

But Patrick was already moving toward the back of the cafeteria at top speed.

Jessica sighed. Bruce Patman hobbled past her on his crutches. Peter Jeffries followed behind him with his lunch tray.

"Hey, Bruce!" Jessica called. "I feel really bad about your foot. Why don't you let me tell you a good fortune to make up for it?"

Bruce turned. "Are you kidding? If I let you tell my fortune, you'll probably do something to my other foot!"

"I don't have that kind of power," Jessica said.

"I'm not taking any chances," Bruce said. He continued on to his table.

Jessica stifled a groan. Wouldn't *someone* trust her enough to let her tell another fortune?

At that moment Cammie Adams stepped forward. "All right," she said. "I am having the *worst* day. If you're sure you're telling good fortunes, I'll let you tell mine."

Jessica was a little disappointed that somebody more popular hadn't stepped forward, but she couldn't be choosy. "OK," she said, leading Cammie to a table in the middle of the cafeteria.

"This is going to be a *good* fortune, right?" Cammie asked with hesitation.

"The best," Jessica assured her. "I promise!"

Jessica grabbed Cammie's hands. She noticed every face in the cafeteria was turned to her. *I'd better make the most of this,* she told herself.

She closed her eyes and concentrated. *Good thoughts,* she reminded herself. *Good thoughts.* "I definitely see something good in your future, Cammie," Jessica said.

"You do? What?"

Jessica opened one eye. A small crowd had gathered. Jessica shivered with delight. She closed her eye again. "I see . . . a prize? Yeah, that's it. A prize. You're going to win a prize, Cammie."

"What sort of prize?" Cammie asked.

Jessica wrinkled her forehead, trying to see more clearly. "I don't know. I can't tell."

Cammie grinned. "Wow. I've never won anything before. That would be so great if you're right, Jessica."

"I will be right," Jessica promised. "You'll see."

"Do you want to tell my fortune, too, Jessica?" Randy Mason stepped forward as Cammie went to sit down.

Great, Jessica thought. *Another nerd.* But what could she do? "Sure! Step right up."

"It's going to be a good one, right?" Randy asked.

"Yes!" Jessica said impatiently. "I told you. Madame

Jessica only sees good things now." She took Randy's hands and closed her eyes. "Yes, this is definitely good." Jessica smiled. "You're going to get out of class early today, Randy. I'm not sure which class, and I'm not sure why. But I definitely see you leaving early."

"Wish I'd gotten that one," Jessica heard Jerry McAllister mutter.

"Me too," Bruce Patman added, stepping forward and pushing Randy out of the way. "It's my turn now."

"Then mine," Jerry added.

Jessica smiled. There was quite a crowd clustered around her. She was back. And she was more popular than ever!

"I hate volleyball," Cammie Adams groaned. She stood across from Jessica on the opposite side of the net.

No wonder, Jessica thought. *She's lousy at it!*

Whenever someone hit the ball toward Cammie, she'd hit it into the net and then grab her arm and cry "Ow!" That, or she'd miss the ball completely.

"Come on, Cammie." Lila Fowler rolled her eyes. "The ball's not going to kill you."

Cammie looked as if she wanted to drop through the floor. Jessica felt a little sorry for her. She also figured that she owed Cammie one. After all, Cammie was the first person who let Jessica tell her fortune that day at lunch. So when it was her turn to serve, Jessica served Cammie a really light ball.

But instead of hitting the ball over the net, Cammie awkwardly whacked it into Belinda Layton's head.

"Cammie!" Belinda yelled.

Jessica cringed.

"Sorry," Cammie whispered.

Belinda rubbed her head. "Jessica, didn't you say Cammie was going to get a prize? I say we award her the booby prize!"

"I second the nomination!" Lila shouted.

Cammie looked like she was ready to cry. "Thanks a lot, Jessica," she said, turning to leave the court.

"Wait a minute!" Jessica cried. "This is not my fault! You're still going to get a good prize. Really!"

But Cammie kept on walking.

"Jessica? Do you have the answer?" Ms. Wyler asked during math class.

Jessica stared at her homework. She hadn't actually gotten around to finishing the assignment last night, and she hadn't been able to concentrate in class. She kept thinking about what had happened to Cammie during gym last period.

"Uh, which question again?" Jessica asked.

But before Ms. Wyler could answer, Randy Mason suddenly started making horrible wheezing noises. Jessica turned and gasped. Randy's lips were turning blue!

He struggled to his feet. His entire body was heaving. His breath was coming in loud, high-pitched gasps.

Ms. Wyler rushed toward him. "Randy? Are you all right?"

"Hey, man," Jerry McAllister said, shoving his desk away. "Are you going to hurl?"

"No, he's not going to hurl," Lloyd Benson replied.

"Can't you see he's having an asthma attack?"

"Does he have an inhaler?" Sophia Rizzo asked. "My cousin has asthma, and she always carries an inhaler."

Randy continued to heave. Sweat poured down his face.

"Somebody help him!" Jessica cried with alarm.

Ms. Wyler dashed to her phone. "Hello, office? I've got a kid here who's having an asthma attack. I need some help!"

"Do you feel better now?" the school nurse asked, touching Randy's arm.

He nodded. He was seated at his desk, breathing into an inhaler. The color was slowly returning to his face.

"Why don't you come down to my office," the nurse suggested as she carefully helped him to his feet. "We'll call your mom and see if she can come and get you."

"Randy really *is* getting out of class early," Jerry McAllister said with amazement.

"Just like Jessica said," Lila pointed out.

Suddenly all heads whirled around to face Jessica.

"Boy, you sure tell *good* fortunes, Jessica," Bruce Patman said.

"I'm glad I didn't let her tell my fortune today," Patrick Morris muttered.

"Me too," Aaron Dallas added as the bell rang.

"But I—this isn't—I mean," Jessica stammered, but everyone was already hurrying out of the room.

"Cheer up, Jessica," Janet Howell said to Jessica with a smirk. She was standing by the lockers with

Belinda Layton and Ellen Riteman when Jessica came out into the hall. "I still don't believe you're pyschic."

"You don't?" Jessica said. For once, she was actually glad to hear that.

Janet shook her head. "No, I don't," she said. "I think you're cursing everyone."

Jessica felt as if she'd been socked in the stomach. But what if Janet was right? What if she *was* somehow cursing everyone?

"Come on, girls," Janet said to the other Unicorns. "Let's go. If we stand here with Jessica too much longer, something bad is going to happen to us, too."

They all turned and walked away. Jessica stared helplessly at their retreating backs. *This was a nightmare. An absolute nightmare!*

Ten

"Is something wrong, Elizabeth?" Ms. Luster asked. "You seem preoccupied today."

Elizabeth pasted a smile on her face. "I'm fine, Ms. Luster." It was Saturday morning, the second day of the Sweet Valley Middle School Fair. Elizabeth was too ashamed to tell Ms. Luster what was bothering her. She was too ashamed to tell *anyone*.

"You're sure?"

Elizabeth nodded. She wished Ms. Luster would go to the bathroom or something. Elizabeth had her copy of *Black Beauty* in her backpack, ready to toss it in with the other returns as soon as she was sure no one was looking.

"Well, if it's OK with you, I think I'll go get a cup of coffee," Ms. Luster said as she grabbed her purse from the shelf under the counter.

Elizabeth sat up a little straighter. "Sure, that's fine. Go right ahead," she said. Amy wasn't due to help out until noon. So once Ms. Luster was gone, Elizabeth would have the booth to herself.

"I'll be back in about fifteen minutes," Ms. Luster promised.

"Take all the time you need," Elizabeth said cheerfully. This was just the break she needed.

Elizabeth waited until Ms. Luster had disappeared into the crowd. Then she jumped down from her stool and reached for her backpack. Her fingers were so shaky, she could hardly grasp the zipper on her pack.

"Is this where we return the overdue library books?" a voice interrupted her.

Elizabeth jumped. Her head banged against the counter. "Ow," she said, rubbing her head as she stood up.

"You OK?" Patrick Morris asked with concern.

Elizabeth smiled. "Yeah, I just bumped my head. Do you have an overdue library book?" she asked.

Patrick sheepishly handed over a science fiction novel. "It's a couple weeks overdue," he admitted.

"Two weeks isn't so bad," Elizabeth said as she took the book from Patrick.

"Yeah, I heard some people have returned books that are several *years* overdue," he said, shaking his head with disbelief.

Elizabeth forced a smile. "It's true. Can you believe the nerve of some people?" She giggled nervously.

"Really!" Patrick returned her smile. "Listen," he said, clearing his throat. "When I first checked this out, Sophia said she wanted to read it. Maybe when you check it in, you can put it aside for her or something."

"I'll do that," Elizabeth promised.

"Good."

Elizabeth set the book with the others that needed to be returned to the middle school library. Then she reached for her backpack. But just as she was about to open it, she noticed Patrick was still standing there.

"Did you need something else?" Elizabeth asked.

"Uh, no." He looked at his feet. "I guess not."

Elizabeth cocked her head. "Are you sure? You look like you've got something on your mind."

Patrick glanced nervously around him. "Well," he said. "I was kind of wondering about Sophia. Has she, uh, you know, mentioned me at all?"

Poor Patrick, Elizabeth thought. She wished she could tell him Sophia had asked about him. "To tell you the truth, I've been so busy with this library amnesty project, I haven't seen much of her."

Patrick sighed. "I can't believe I forgot her birthday. What am I going to do, Elizabeth?"

Elizabeth looked at him sympathetically. "You could try bringing her flowers or something," she suggested.

"Hey, that's a good idea!" Patrick's whole face lit up. "Do you think she'd forgive me if I did that?"

"Probably," Elizabeth said, glancing around the fair. She wanted to help Patrick, but she was starting to get nervous. Ms. Luster would be returning soon. She didn't have much time to return her book.

"I think there are some seventh-graders selling flowers somewhere around here," Elizabeth told Patrick. "Why don't you see if you can find them?"

Patrick leaned on the counter as he glanced over his shoulder. "Well, maybe I could give her something *better* than flowers," he said thoughtfully. "Look over there."

Elizabeth looked. "What?" she asked. All she saw was the basketball free-throw booth.

"Do you see the prizes over there?" Patrick asked. "Those are the biggest stuffed animals at the whole fair. Do you think Sophia would like one?"

"Sure. Who wouldn't?" Elizabeth shifted her weight from one foot to the other. She really had to get her book returned.

"Then that settles it," Patrick said. "I'm going to win one for Sophia."

"Great idea, Patrick," Elizabeth said. Privately she thought it would take an awful lot of free throws to win, but she didn't have time to get into that.

Once he was gone, Elizabeth reached for her backpack again and quickly unzipped it.

"Hey, Elizabeth!" Aaron Dallas banged his hands on the counter.

The noise startled her and she dropped her backpack.

"This is my grandma Dallas," Aaron said, pointing at the woman beside him. "Grandma, this is Elizabeth Wakefield."

Elizabeth and Aaron's grandmother smiled politely at each other.

"Grandma's got a book that was due way back in 1962!" Aaron said. "Can you believe it?"

Elizabeth's eyes widened in amazement when she saw the title of the book Aaron's grandma had. *Black Beauty!*

"It was my favorite book as a child," Mrs. Dallas said as she clasped the book to her chest.

"Mine too," Elizabeth croaked.

"Has anybody returned a book that was more overdue than that?" Aaron asked hopefully.

"I, uh, don't think so," Elizabeth said. She opened the record book and scanned the date due column. "No, the most overdue book we've received so far was due in 1966."

"All right!" Aaron cried. "You'll share your pizza with me, won't you, Grandma?" he asked while Mrs. Dallas filled in the record book.

"We'll see," she told him. Then she turned to Elizabeth. "I can't tell you how embarrassed I am to be returning this after so many years."

"Oh, I can imagine how you must feel," Elizabeth said.

"It's shameful, really. Even more shameful to think I may get a prize for returning it." She laughed.

Elizbeth started to laugh, too, but then Ms. Luster returned with a steaming cup of coffee. Elizabeth's heart sank. *So much for returning my overdue book,* she thought.

"Hey, Ms. Luster. This is my grandma Dallas," Aaron said. "She's going to win the free pizza for having the most overdue book. Look how overdue her book is!"

Mrs. Dallas laughed nervously. "Now Aaron, you don't need to tell everybody about this, do you?"

"It's OK, Grandma," Aaron said. "This is the librarian."

Ms. Luster smiled. "It's nice to meet you, Mrs. Dallas. And we appreciate your returning that book after so many years," she said.

Elizabeth slid her backpack farther under the

counter with her foot. At least *one* copy of *Black Beauty* got returned today, she thought miserably.

This is terrible! Jessica thought. *Last week the line circled my booth three times. This week I don't have a line at all.*

Jessica stared miserably at the line that was growing in front of the Unicorn's dunking booth. *What's so great about tossing a ball and knocking a teacher into a pool of Jell-O?* Jessica wondered. It wasn't even real Jell-O. The Unicorns couldn't get that part right. But no one seemed to care. Kids were lining up over there as if it were the greatest booth ever.

"Hey, *Madame* Jessica," Janet taunted her as she walked past. "Where are your crowds?"

Jessica narrowed her eyes at Janet. "They'll be back this afternoon," she said with confidence. She couldn't let Janet see she was worried.

Janet laughed. "Sure, Jessica. Whatever you say. Listen, I'd love to stay and chat, but we're really swamped." She turned to leave, but then doubled back. "Don't take that to mean we want any help from *you*," she added.

"I wouldn't help you anyway," Jessica called after her. But it was hard to tell whether or not Janet even heard.

Jessica was so frustrated, she could hardly stand it. She had to get people to come to her booth again. She just had to! But how?

Maybe if she lowered her price? If all the other booths were fifty cents and hers was less, wouldn't that attract more people? She grabbed a Magic Marker and hurried around to the other side of her booth. She crossed off the 50¢ and wrote 5¢ in its place. Then she went back inside to wait for her customers.

Jessica cracked her fortune cookie open. She'd certainly had plenty of time for lunch today. Time enough for a plate of shrimp chow mein, fried rice, and an egg roll.

Jessica munched the cookie before reading the fortune. She believed you had to do that or the fortune wouldn't come true. As she swallowed the last bits of cookie, she turned the little scrap of paper over. *There is yet time enough for you to take a different path,* it read.

Yeah, right, she thought. *What different path? I've already set up a fortune-telling booth. I can't back out of that now.*

Jessica drummed her nails against her counter. *Well, maybe I could change my fortune-telling strategy again,* she mused. But how? The problem was, her psychic powers were just so much stronger than she ever imagined.

Maybe I should just quit using my powers altogether, she thought. *Yeah, I could just make up the fortunes. I could give the kind of fortune you get in a fortune cookie! Something that sounds old and wise and people can read whatever they want into it. Nothing bad could come from that kind of fortune,* Jessica thought with growing excitement.

Suddenly Jerry McAllister appeared at her window. "Five cents?" he asked. "Really?"

"Really," Jessica said, sitting up a little straighter. Here was her opportunity to try out her new path. "Would you like me to tell your fortune?"

"I guess so," Jerry said. "I was hoping to do the dunk tank, but there's such a long line over there."

"Thanks for pointing that out, Jerry," Jessica said glumly. After a comment like that, she had half a mind to give Jerry a *real* fortune. But she had to prove she wasn't cursing anyone. So she took Jerry's hands and closed her eyes, pretending to feel his psychic energy. "Uh . . . it's better to have tried and failed than to never have tried at all," she told him.

Jerry wrinkled his forehead. "It's better to have tried and failed than to never have tried at all! What kind of fortune is that?"

"One that you should take very seriously," Jessica said. "Madame Jessica is all-knowing and wise."

"I think Madame Jessica is off her rocker," Jerry said.

Between customers, Jessica started to make a list of all the old sayings she could think of. There was "Do unto others"; "Ask not, want not"; "The early bird gets the worm"; "If a task is once begun, never leave it 'til it's done." She was on a roll now.

"Wow! Five cents? Really?" Peter Burns stuck his head in Jessica's window.

Jessica brushed her list off the table. "Yup," she said. "I decided to run a special this week."

"How come?" Peter asked.

Jessica shrugged. "I just felt like it."

"Well, this must be my lucky day," Peter said. "I don't have fifty cents, but I do have five cents." He plunked a nickel down on the counter.

Jessica put the nickel into her change box and took

Peter's hands. "Ask not, want not," she told him in a serious voice.

"What's that supposed to mean?"

Jessica shrugged. "My job is to give the fortune. Yours is to find meaning in it."

"I see why you lowered the price to five cents," Peter muttered as he walked away.

Jessica shrugged. So her fortunes weren't all that exciting anymore. But at least they wouldn't do any more damage to her reputation.

"How much money have we made so far?" Janet asked.

"I don't know," Kimberly replied, running her hand through her thick, dark hair. "A lot."

Janet glanced with satisfaction into the change box as Kimberly added another two quarters to the pile of bills and loose change. They were really doing well today. *Much better than Jessica was*, Janet noted proudly.

"You get three chances to knock Mr. Seigel into the purple pool," Kimberly told Peter Burns as she handed him three baseballs.

"You better let Peter get a little closer," Mr. Seigel yelled from the dunking seat. "The only way he could possibly hit the target is if he came up with a science project that did it for him."

There were snickers from the crowd.

"Very funny, Mr. Seigel," Peter said. He wound up and threw his first ball toward the target. It hit the tarp behind the target with a thud and dropped to the floor.

"Come on, Peter!" Mr. Seigel said. "My three-year-old could hit that target with his eyes closed!"

Peter wound up again and aimed another ball at the target. This one hit the tarp, too.

"Where'd you learn to throw?" Mr. Seigel yelled. "The back of a Cracker Jack box?"

Peter wound up a third time and flung another ball. This one hit the target with a loud *ding!* Mr. Seigel splashed down into the purple pool.

The crowd cheered.

"Ha! Gotcha good, Mr. Seigel!" Peter said with satisfaction as Mr. Seigel smoothed back his wet hair and climbed back up to the chair.

"If you guys think we're doing good this week, just wait until next week when we have Mr. Clark sitting in the dunking seat!" Belinda Layton said.

"No kidding." Janet grinned. It was fun to dunk a science teacher, but to dunk a principal? Kids would probably be camped out on lawn chairs before the fair opened to assure themselves a place in line!

She glanced across the room at Jessica, who was sitting at her booth with her chin in her hands. *Poor Jessica*, Janet thought. *I guess some of us have it and some of us don't.*

"Can I get you another cup of coffee?" Elizabeth asked Ms. Luster.

"I only drink coffee in the morning," Ms. Luster said absently. "But thanks, anyway."

Elizabeth sighed. Ms. Luster hadn't taken a break since that morning, so Elizabeth still hadn't managed to return *Black Beauty*. She figured that the more Ms. Luster drank, the more likely she'd be to take a break.

"Well, how about a soft drink," Elizabeth suggested

eagerly. "A root beer maybe? Or some lemonade?"

Ms. Luster smiled. "Elizabeth, if *you* want to take a break, go ahead. I can hold down the fort."

Elizabeth shook her head. Taking a break would definitely not solve her problem.

She watched Ms. Luster sort through the returned books. Normally Elizabeth was glad that Sweet Valley Middle School had such a dedicated librarian. But at that moment, she wished she weren't quite *so* dedicated.

Jessica stared glumly into her cash box. The fair was ending for the day, and she'd made only twenty cents. Janet would never let her live it down if she found out. *Well, at least no one can accuse me of cursing them,* she reasoned.

She began cleaning up her booth when Jerry McAllister walked by holding his stomach. "I should've known better than to trust you!" he moaned.

"What are you talking about?" Jessica asked. She couldn't remember which fortune she'd given Jerry, but how could anything bad have come from it?

Jerry glared at Jessica. "You said it's better to have tried and failed than never to have tried at all! That means I'm supposed to try new things, right?"

"Sure," Jessica said.

"Well, I tried the pie-eating contest over at Charlie Cashman's booth," he snapped. "Not only did I lose the contest, I feel like I'm going to puke! And it's all *your* fault, Jessica!"

"*My* fault!" Jessica cried.

But Jerry didn't hang around to talk about it. He

Eleven

"Here's that book on TV history," Jerry McAllister said as he slid the book across the returns desk in the library. It was Elizabeth's free period, and she was filing cards for Ms. Luster.

She picked up the book. "Did you find what you needed?" she asked.

"Yes, but never mind that. I just wanted you to be aware that I brought the book back *on time*." He pounded his fist on the counter. "In fact, it's even a few days early! Are you satisfied?"

Elizabeth swallowed hard. "Listen, Jerry. I'm sorry I gave you such a hard time before. I shouldn't have said anything unless you did actually keep it overdue."

"Darn right!" Jerry said.

"Well, would you like to keep the book a little longer?" Elizabeth asked.

Jerry rolled his eyes. "My report is finished. Why

kept right on walking, practically colliding with Elizabeth.

Elizabeth glanced from Jerry to Jessica. "What's bugging him?" she asked.

Jessica put her hand to her forehead. "The same thing that's bugging everyone else. Me!"

"Oh, Jessica, it's not that bad," Elizabeth said.

"Yes, it is," Jessica insisted. "No one's even talking to me anymore." She crossed her arms in front her. "Everyone's afraid of me. They're afraid of my psychic power."

"Well, you're the one who always wanted to be psychic," Elizabeth pointed out. "It looks like you got your wish."

"I never *wanted* to be," Jessica protested. "I just always knew I was. But now I wish I wasn't. You can't imagine what a terrible burden it is, Lizzie."

"Oh, Jessica." Elizabeth sighed.

would I want to keep it any longer? You are really weird, Elizabeth!"

Elizabeth sighed. *Not weird*, she thought. *Just irresponsible.*

At the moment, *her* library record was worse than Jerry's.

As Jessica passed Jerry McAllister, Peter Burns, and Charlie Cashman in the hallway at lunchtime, they all looked at her as though she had leprosy. She dashed around the corner and out the back door before they had a chance to accuse her of cursing them with her psychic powers.

The situation was desperate, she decided. She'd have to eat her lunch alone.

There was a tall orange tree a few feet from the door. Jessica could sit on the opposite side and no one would be able to see her from the school. But to her surprise, she found Elizabeth seated under the tree when she got there. "What are *you* doing here?" Jessica asked her sister.

Elizabeth jumped. "Oh, you scared me, Jess!"

"Sorry," Jessica replied as she dropped to the ground beside Elizabeth. "So what are you doing out here, anyway?" she repeated as she started unwrapping her sandwich.

Elizabeth shrugged. "Thinking," she replied. "What are you doing out here?"

"Thinking," Jessica echoed. She took a bite of her peanut butter sandwich. Then she took a deep breath. "Tell me the truth, Elizabeth. Do you think I could somehow be cursing everyone?"

"Of course not," Elizabeth responded, staring off into space.

"I'm starting to think I am," Jessica went on as she pulled the crusts off her sandwich. "All my fortunes come true. No matter what, they always come true. And even if I mean them to be good fortunes, they turn out bad."

"It's just coincidence," Elizabeth said.

Jessica stared at her sister. Somehow Elizabeth wasn't as convincing as she usually was. It was as if she were a million miles away. "Is something the matter, Elizabeth?" she asked.

"Oh, Jess," Elizabeth cried, finally meeting her sister's eyes. "I did a terrible thing."

Jessica looked at her curiously. Elizabeth *never* did anything terrible. "What did you do?" she asked.

"I found an overdue library book behind my dresser," she said shamefully.

"So?" Jessica shrugged.

"So, I checked it out in *second grade*," Elizabeth said.

Jessica waited for the terrible part. But Elizabeth didn't say anything else. "You mean, that's it?" Jessica asked incredulously. "That's the terrible thing? You found an overdue library book behind your dresser?"

Elizabeth nodded. She stared at the ground.

Jessica laughed. "Elizabeth, come on! It's not like you kept it on purpose. You can return it at your library amnesty booth on Saturday, and you won't even have to pay a fine."

Elizabeth shook her head sadly. "How can I do that after all the trouble I've been giving other kids for having overdue books?"

Jessica looked at her sister blankly. "You just put

your book in with all the other overdue books. I mean, who cares whether you've had a book since second grade? Nobody's going to stop talking to you over it. But look at me. Everybody hates me."

"Nobody hates you, Jessica," Elizabeth said. "People are just a little nervous. But they'll come around. You'll see. You're not responsible for everything that goes wrong in the world."

"How do you know?" Jessica asked. "Maybe I am."

"Hi, Elizabeth," Patrick Morris said, coming up to Elizabeth in the library. "I'm returning the books I checked out for my social studies paper."

"You can put them in the book drop," Elizabeth said. "Either Ms. Luster or I will see that they're checked in today."

Elizabeth had been devoting almost all her free time to the library. Working there made her feel better about her overdue book. She felt like she was working off the fine.

"Great," Patrick said as he slid the books through the book drop. As he was leaving, Sophia came in. Sophia and Patrick looked at each other, then they both continued on their way.

Sophia went to the rack of paperbacks. Elizabeth watched as she kept spinning it and spinning it, without taking a book.

"Is something the matter, Sophia?" Elizabeth asked. "Are you upset about Patrick?"

Sophia let out a huge breath. "I miss him," she said sadly, raising her eyes to meet Elizabeth's. "I'm still mad that he forgot my birthday, but I miss him."

Elizabeth touched Sophia's arm. "Maybe you should talk to him," she said.

"I don't know." Sophia looked away. "We said some terrible things. I don't know if they can be taken back."

"I bet they can," Elizabeth said. "I happen to know for a fact that Patrick misses you, too."

"Really?" Sophia asked wide-eyed. "How do you know?"

"I just do," Elizabeth replied, thinking back to the fair last Saturday and how Patrick wanted so badly to win a stuffed animal for Sophia. *He must not have been able to do it*, she thought sadly.

"Well, what should I say to him the next time I see him?" Sophia asked.

Elizabeth shrugged. "I don't know. Why don't you just say hi and go from there?"

"I'll think about it," Sophia said. Then she turned back to the rack of books.

Elizabeth continued her shelving. She hoped Sophia and Patrick would work things out. Not only because they seemed miserable without each other, but because it would reverse one of Jessica's predictions. Maybe if that happened, people would realize Jessica wasn't cursing anyone.

"Geez, what's with you guys?" Steven asked as he opened the refrigerator door. Jessica had just gotten home from school and was sitting at the kitchen table drowning her sorrows in a huge bowl of ice cream.

"Hmm?" Jessica mumbled absently, licking the ice cream off her spoon and staring blankly out the window.

Steven closed the refrigerator. "You're moping around in here, and Elizabeth is moping in the family room. I mean, you should see it. You'd think all her friends were moving to China or something."

Jessica glanced at her brother, who grabbed a box of cookies from the pantry. "Actually, her problem is totally nothing. My problem is much more serious."

"Well then, maybe you two should just switch problems," he said as he left the kitchen with the whole box of cookies.

Switch problems? Jessica thought. An idea began to take shape in her head. She slammed her palm down on the table. Why hadn't she thought of that herself?

"Elizabeth!" Jessica yelled as she tore into the family room. "I've got the perfect solution to both our problems!"

Elizabeth looked up from her homework. "What?" she asked glumly.

"We can switch places at the fair next week!" Jessica announced. "I could pretend to be you at the library booth, and you could be Madame Jessica!"

Elizabeth frowned. "What are you talking about, Jess? What would be the point?"

"You can sit in my booth and pretend to be me," Jessica explained excitedly. "Only none of your fortunes would come true because *you're* not psychic. So when your fortunes don't come true, people will realize I'm not cursing anyone and things will get back to normal."

Elizabeth wrinkled her brow. "I don't think so, Jess," she said. "I really don't want to be a fortune-teller."

Jessica looked Elizabeth straight in the eye.

Elizabeth was certainly being exasperating. But Jessica had a feeling she knew a way she could change her sister's mind. "You know," she said slowly, "if you're me and I'm you, I'll return your overdue book for you."

Elizabeth's eyes widened. "You will?"

Jessica smiled, a glint coming into her eye. "No prob."

Elizabeth chewed on her bottom lip while she thought about it. "Well . . . OK," she said finally.

Jessica jumped up and threw her arms around her sister. "All right!" she cried. "This is going to work out, Elizabeth. You'll see. Come Saturday, both our problems will be solved."

Twelve

"Where's Mr. Clark?" Jerry McAllister demanded when he reached the Unicorns' dunking tank on Saturday morning. He had a wad of bills scrunched in his hand. "I've been waiting for this all week!"

Janet smiled nervously. Mr. Clark was supposed to have arrived ten minutes before. So far there was no sign of him. "He should be here soon," she said with forced optimism.

"I'll wait," Jerry said.

"So will I," Bruce Patman said as he leaned on his crutches.

Within ten minutes a line stretched all the way from the dunk tank to the door.

"What's the holdup over here?" Ms. Langberg, the girls' gym coach, asked as she walked up to Janet.

"Mr. Clark hasn't shown up yet," Janet explained.

"We don't have anybody to sit in the dunk tank," Lila added.

"You mean this line isn't moving at all?" Ms. Langberg asked as she turned to see how far back the line went.

"Not at the moment," Lila admitted.

Ms. Langberg glanced out over the crowd. "Well, I picked up the swim team's swim suits at the cleaners yesterday. I've still got them in my car, if one of you wants to put one on and sit up there until Mr. Clark gets here," she offered.

"You've got to be kidding!" Janet said. She wasn't sure which would be worse, wearing somebody else's swim suit or sitting over a tank full of watery Jell-O, waiting to get dunked.

Suddenly the crowd erupted in shouts. "Come on! We want a dunker! We want a dunker!"

"Maybe one of us *should* get up there," Mandy said weakly. "These kids have been waiting for quite a while."

Janet frowned. "*Unicorns* should not be dunked in watery Jell-O. Think about our reputation."

Mary glanced anxiously at the crowd. "We wouldn't have to sit there very long. Mr. Clark should be here any minute."

Janet sighed. "Oh, all right. So why don't you go sit up there, Ellen?"

"Me?" Ellen turned pale.

"I think the only fair thing would be to draw straws," Mary said quickly.

"I definitely agree!" Ellen exclaimed, looking relieved.

"Well, fine," Janet said. She and Lila went over to the hot-dog booth and grabbed a bunch of straws. They cut them all different lengths. Then Janet lined them all up in her hands so no one could see the bottoms. "OK," she said. "Whoever draws the shortest one has to sit in the dunking chair."

"How come you get to hold the straws?" Ellen asked.

"Because I'm not going to draw one," Janet explained. "I'm going to go call Mr. Clark and make sure he's on his way."

"OK, I'll pick first," Tamara said. She drew a medium-length straw. "Phew," she sighed with relief.

Mandy also drew a medium-length straw.

So did Ellen.

Then Lila took her turn. Her mouth dropped as she stared at her short straw. "Oh, no," she groaned. "I want a redraw. There were only three left to choose from."

"No way," Tamara said. "We agreed to draw straws. It was the only fair way to decide."

Lila glared at Tamara. "I'm only sitting up there for ten minutes," she said angrily. "If Mr. Clark isn't here by then, someone else is going to have to take my place."

"We'll cross that bridge when we come to it," Janet said. "Now why don't you go and get a suit from Ms. Langberg, and I'll go call Mr. Clark."

"I don't know, maybe I should return the book myself," Elizabeth said with a worried frown. She and Jessica were behind the Madame Jessica booth, getting Elizabeth dressed up to play the part.

"Would you relax!" Jessica said. "I can return your book for you. It's not a big deal."

"Well, what are you going to tell Ms. Luster about it?"

Jessica shrugged. "I'll think of something."

"That's what I'm afraid of," Elizabeth muttered. She fluffed the sleeves on her dress and adjusted her scarves. She didn't know how Jessica managed to breathe with all those itchy scarves around her neck.

"Stop scratching!" Jessica said, grabbing Elizabeth's hands and pulling them down. "People won't think you're Madame Jessica if you're constantly pulling at your clothes."

"I'm *not* Madame Jessica," Elizabeth reminded her sister.

"Come on, Lizzie," Jessica said. "We always have fun when we trade places."

"But I'm not really trading places with you," Elizabeth pointed out. "I'm trading places with *Madame Jessica*. And I have no idea who *she* is!"

Jessica pushed a couple strands of Elizabeth's hair behind her shoulder. "You'll do fine," she insisted. "All you have to do is make up a few fortunes. Any old fortunes! As long as nothing bad happens to anybody as a result. My entire life depends on you, Lizzie!"

"Great," Elizabeth said. "As long as there's no pressure."

SPLASH! Lila stood up in the pool and wiped her face. "All right! That's it!" she cried as she climbed the ladder out of the pool. "That's three times I've been dunked. I've had it! Somebody else can sit up there for a while!"

She dashed to the girls' bathroom before Janet could say a word.

"So who's going to sit up there now?" Ellen asked.

"We want a dunker! We want a dunker!" the crowd chanted.

"Why don't you guys draw straws again," Janet said quickly. "I'm going to try calling Mr. Clark again."

Mandy started to say something to her, but Janet was already hurrying away. There had been no answer at Mr. Clark's house before, so Janet couldn't imagine she'd get an answer now. But at least calling him gave her something to do. And an excuse to get away when the other Unicorns were drawing straws.

"Good morning, Ms. Luster," Jessica said cheerfully, trying her best to sound like Elizabeth.

"There you are!" Ms. Luster said as she glanced up from the morning newspaper. "I was wondering where you were this morning."

Jessica thought about what Elizabeth would say if she happened to show up late for something. Probably she'd just tell the truth. "I was helping Jessica get dressed," Jessica-as-Elizabeth said. "It takes her a while to put all those scarves on."

Ms. Luster smiled. "I suppose it does."

Jessica reached into Elizabeth's backpack and pulled out *Black Beauty*. She had prepared a sob story about how she-as-Elizabeth had lent the book to a friend who'd moved away, and how she'd tried and tried to get ahold of the friend to get the book back. She didn't quite have an ending for the story yet, but she knew something would come to her once she started talking. "I, uh, also wanted to return this," she said.

Ms. Luster raised an eyebrow. "It's overdue?" she asked with surprise.

"Yeah. I—" Jessica began.

"Just put it with the others," Ms. Luster said with a wave of her hand. Then she turned back to her newspaper.

Just put it with the others? Jessica gaped at Ms. Luster. Did that mean she wouldn't get to tell her sob story?

Apparently, it did. Ms. Luster obviously couldn't have cared less about Elizabeth's overdue book.

I told *Elizabeth she didn't have to worry*, Jessica thought. *Hey, there's one thing I predicted that turned out good!*

"Mr. Clark called to say he's been delayed," Ms. Langberg said as she walked over to the Unicorn booth. "He'll try and get here as soon as he can."

Janet groaned to herself. "Well, just how delayed is he?" she asked. "We've got people waiting for him."

"Oh, I don't mind," Bruce Patman said as he stepped up to take his turn in line. "I knocked Lila in your pool. I knocked Mary in. Now I'm going to knock Ellen in. Not bad for a guy on crutches, is it? Maybe I'll get lucky and knock every single Unicorn in before the day is over!"

Janet glared at him. "Don't count on it," she said between clenched teeth.

"This is getting ridiculous!" Janet cried. An hour had passed and Mr. Clark still hadn't shown up. Wasn't he always lecturing kids about following through?

Janet paced back and forth in front of the dunk tank. True, theirs was still the most popular booth.

But she didn't like seeing her friends sitting in the dunking chair. Unicorns did not belong in dunking chairs!

Kimberly Haver was sitting in the dunking chair now. Nearly every Unicorn had already taken a turn. Pretty soon Kimberly was going to decide she's had enough. Then who would get up there? *I've got to get out of here*, Janet thought.

Because there was *one* Unicorn who absolutely, positively did not belong in the dunking chair: Janet herself.

"Ho hum." Elizabeth yawned. She wished she'd brought a book. She'd been sitting in the Madame Jessica booth for over an hour, and she hadn't had a single customer. She'd never been so bored in her life.

She was tapping her nails against the counter when she noticed someone wearing jeans and a crisp white blouse crouched low around the side of the booth. It was Janet Howell!

"What are you doing?" Elizabeth asked her.

Janet jumped. She glanced warily back toward the dunking booth. "Uh, nothing."

Elizabeth was about to ask if Janet happened to have a book on her, when she remembered she was Jessica. *What would Jessica say to Janet?* She tossed her hair to get into the Jessica-mood. "So I heard you guys have been sitting in the dunk tank."

"Yes," Janet said in a tired voice. "Mr. Clark was supposed to do it, but nobody knows where he is."

"Too bad," Elizabeth-as-Jessica said. "You must not have had your turn yet. Your hair looks too good."

Janet's cheeks reddened. She ran her hand through her hair. "No, I haven't," she snapped. "And I'm not *going* to have a turn if I can help it."

Elizabeth raised an eyebrow. "Just how do you plan to *avoid* sitting up there if the other Unicorns have all had a turn?"

Janet glanced worriedly over her shoulder. "I just will." She turned back to face Elizabeth. "So, how's it going with you, Jessica?" she asked with a fake smile.

Elizabeth frowned. Since when does Janet care how it's going with anybody other than herself?

Janet moved a little closer to Jessica's booth and glanced over her shoulder again. Elizabeth followed her gaze. She was looking toward the Unicorns' booth. But you couldn't see much of it from here.

Maybe that was the idea, Elizabeth realized suddenly. Janet was going to avoid her turn in the dunk tank by hiding out at Madame Jessica's.

Oh, Jessica would love this, Elizabeth thought. *Janet's not so great and powerful when she's slinking around like a snake.* Jessica would certainly take advantage of this moment. And it was Elizabeth's duty, as Madame Jessica, to do exactly what Jessica would do.

She cleared her throat. "You can't just stand here and block my window, Janet. That is unless you want to have your fortune told."

Janet glared at Elizabeth. "Oh, all right," she said. She turned around in her seat. "What do I have to do?"

"Well, first you have to pay," Elizabeth said. "Fifty cents."

"Fifty cents!" Janet cried. "The sign says five cents."

"OK, five cents," Elizabeth agreed.

Janet opened her purse and pulled out five pennies.

She plunked them down on the counter. "There! Now what?"

"Sit down," Elizabeth said. Janet sat and Elizabeth reached for her hands. "I see . . . your white blouse," Elizabeth intoned. "Your beautiful white blouse."

"Of course you do," Janet said. "I'm wearing it!"

Elizabeth brought her hands to her face in pretend shock. "Why, I see a stain on it. Isn't that a shame?" she asked sweetly.

"W-w-what do you mean?" Janet asked in a panicked voice as she glanced down at her blouse. "What kind of stain? Where's it going to come from?"

Elizabeth scrunched her face up as though she were trying to see the vision more clearly. "Well, I can't tell you what the stain is, but it's very big and very bright. I mean, I'm probably standing fifty feet away from you and I can see it perfectly!"

Janet narrowed her eyes and stood up abruptly. "If that fortune comes true," she said in a harsh whisper, "you're dead!"

Thirteen

"So she didn't even blink when you returned *Black Beauty*?" Elizabeth asked incredulously.

"Nope," Jessica replied with satisfaction. "Piece of cake."

Elizabeth sighed with relief. Jessica had joined her in the Madame Jessica booth a few minutes earlier, and already Elizabeth was feeling tons better than she had that morning. She could hardly wait to tell her sister about giving Janet the scare of her life. Quickly she filled her in on the details about the dunking booth and telling Janet's fortune.

"I told her she was going to get a stain on her pretty new blouse," Elizabeth finished, pleased with herself.

"Elizabeth!" Jessica cried. "How could you? The last thing I need is trouble with Janet Howell!"

Elizabeth jumped at her sister's sharp tone. "But— I mean, I thought you guys were so competitive with each other. Didn't you want to get back at Janet for some of the mean things she's done?"

Jessica buried her head in her hands. "Yeah, but not like this. She could accuse me of cursing her and I'd be ruined. Ruined!"

Elizabeth put her hand on her sister's shoulder. "Come on, Jessica. You said it yourself: I'm not psychic. It's not like the fortune is going to come true."

"Yeah, well, we'd better make sure of that." Jessica pulled the curtain to her booth closed and quickly untied Elizabeth's scarves.

"What are you doing?" Elizabeth asked.

"I'm helping you out of this getup," Jessica explained. "I don't want you to trip on a scarf or anything on the way."

"On the way where?" Elizabeth asked. "Where are we going?"

"We're going to follow Janet Howell." Jessica stood up, clutching her sister's arm. "And we're going to make sure no stain gets anywhere near her blouse."

"Um, Sophia?"

Sophia was wandering over to the Unicorns' booth when she heard someone calling her name. She turned. Patrick was standing behind her, carrying a huge pink bear and a bouquet of flowers. "These are for you," he said shyly.

Sophia stared at him blankly. "What—what are these?"

"They're flowers and a bear," Patrick explained.

"Well, yeah, I can see that." Sophia cleared her throat. "But I mean—what are they for?"

Patrick looked down at his feet. "I'm really sorry I forgot your birthday, Sophia. I've actually got a real present for you at home. Just in case I wasn't able to make enough free throws to win you a bear."

"You won this making free throws?" Sophia asked with surprise. Patrick wasn't exactly known for being a great basketball player.

Patrick nodded proudly. "I've been practicing in my driveway until after dark every night."

"You have?" Sophia's heart was beating quickly. No one had ever gone to so much trouble for her before.

"I know this doesn't make up for the fact that I forgot your birthday, but, well, I hope you'll accept them anyway," Patrick continued softly.

Sophia smiled and took the flowers and stuffed bear. "I guess I kind of overreacted about you forgetting my birthday."

Patrick shook his head. "No you didn't. I shouldn't have forgotten it."

"No, I—" Sophia broke off and grinned sheepishly. "We're arguing again."

"Well," Patrick said. "Why don't we just stop?"

"There she is!" Jessica hissed. The twins ducked behind a garbage can as Janet stopped by the hot-dog booth and scratched her leg.

Elizabeth giggled. "I feel like a character in one of my Amanda Howard mysteries."

Jessica frowned. "This is serious, Elizabeth. You don't mess around with Janet Howell."

As Janet started walking again, Jessica and Elizabeth crept along behind her. After several feet,

Janet stopped and looked all around her.

"Duck!" Jessica commanded, pulling Elizabeth behind the cotton-candy stand.

Elizabeth was breathing hard. "Why does she keep stopping, anyway? It's like she expects someone to jump out of the shadows at her."

"She's probably worried someone's going to jump out and stain her blouse," Jessica whispered.

When she came to the end of a long string of booths, Janet flattened herself against the wall and slowly peered around the corner.

Just then one of the back doors opened and Sarah Thomas walked out loaded down with three buckets of paint. Sarah teetered toward Janet, struggling with her load. Suddenly Janet whirled around. She started back toward Sarah, without really watching where she was going. Jessica felt her breath catch in her throat.

"No!" Jessica yelled as she ran toward Sarah. She wasn't sure who collided with whom. All she knew was, there was suddenly red, yellow, and blue paint *everywhere*!

Jessica blinked as paint dribbled down her hair and onto her shoulders and clothes.

"Look at this mess!" Elizabeth cried. She was also covered with paint. So was the wall behind her. So was the floor. And so was Sarah Thomas.

Jessica felt her heart sink with dread. Slowly she turned toward Janet—and gasped. It was a miracle! There were a couple splatters of paint on Janet's jeans, but somehow her white blouse had managed to stay white!

Elizabeth noticed Janet's blouse at exactly the same moment. "I don't believe it," she clasped her hands to her cheeks. "Janet! Your blouse!"

Janet glared at Elizabeth and glanced down at her blouse. Her mouth dropped open. "It's still clean!" she cried.

Jessica's whole face was glowing as she turned toward the gathering crowd. "The curse is broken!" she shouted. Then she beamed at Janet. "I told you your blouse would be stained, and it's about the only thing here that *isn't* stained! You should thank me, Janet."

Janet shot Jessica a withering look. "Don't push it, Jessica."

"It *is* pretty incredible that your blouse didn't get stained, Janet," Sarah pointed out.

"Yeah, I thought Jessica was supposed to be such bad luck," Aaron Dallas replied.

"Jessica's not bad luck!" Elizabeth defended her sister. "All of her predictions were nothing but silly coincidences."

"Yeah, look at Anna!" Cammie Adams said. "Her jacket was never really lost. Someone picked it up, and it was in the office all this time."

Jessica turned around to face Anna, who was proudly wearing her new leather jacket.

"And Sophia and I are back together." Smiling, Patrick Morris held up his hand, which was clasped with Sophia's.

"See?" Jessica spoke up. "I'm not really bad luck. Just because I can see into the future—"

"That's enough talk about fortunes and seeing into the future," Ms. Langberg broke in, pushing her way to the front of the crowd.

"No kidding," Janet muttered.

"What I want to know is, who's going to get a

mop over here and start cleaning up this mess?" Ms. Langberg asked.

"Not me." Bruce Patman held up a purple ticket. "I've still got a ticket for the dunking booth, and I intend to use it before the fair is over!"

Janet glanced at Lila, Ellen, Mandy, and Tamara. "Well, what are you guys waiting for? Shouldn't you be manning the booth?"

Lila folded her arms. "Actually, we've all already had a turn in the dunking chair."

"But there's still one person who hasn't." Mandy looked at Janet meaningfully.

Janet flushed. "Well, as president of the Unicorns, I don't think it's my duty—"

"Oh, no," Tamara shook her head. "It's *every* member's duty." She grabbed one of Janet's arms. "The rest of us have already taken a turn. It's *your* turn now!"

"You can't get out of it, Janet." Lila stepped forward and grabbed Janet's other arm.

Janet glared at Tamara and Lila. "Whose stupid idea was it to have a dunk tank anyway?" she asked as the two led her away.

Jessica and Elizabeth grinned at each other. "I wonder whose?" Jessica said.

I'd better not end up in there, Janet thought, looking down at the murky purple pool beneath her.

She glanced at the kids who were in line. Bruce Patman was up first. He handed his crutches to Jerry McAllister to hold while he took a ball from Mandy Miller. He looked up at Janet and grinned as he tossed the baseball from one hand to the other.

Janet swallowed hard. "You don't really want to dunk me, Bruce," she told him. "You and I go back a long way."

Bruce laughed. "Yeah, back to when I was in kindergarten and you were in first grade. And you made me eat sand!" He wound up and flung the ball at the target.

Miss!

Janet watched as the ball rolled back across the floor. Mandy picked it up and handed it back to Bruce.

"I'm sorry I made you eat sand," Janet said desperately. "But that was a long time ago. Can't you forgive me?"

Bruce threw another ball.

He missed again.

As he held up his third baseball, Janet glanced at the clock on the side wall. Fortunately the day was going to be over in about fifteen minutes. And it looked as though Janet would avoid getting dunked.

"Having fun, Janet?"

Janet looked down to see Jessica, her cheeks and clothes smeared with paint, waving at her.

"What are you doing here?" Janet asked. "I thought you were supposed to be cleaning up."

"I did," Jessica said. "Elizabeth and Sarah can handle the rest without me." Then she turned and whispered something to Bruce. He laughed.

Janet was so angry, she was ready to scream. "Are you going to throw that ball or not?" she called to Bruce.

Bruce wound up for his final throw. He missed again. Janet let out her breath in a sigh of relief. "Too bad, Patman," she said smugly. "It looks like you're losing your touch."

Bruce reached into his pocket. "Well, I've still got fifty cents left. I'll just have to go to the back of the line and try again!"

Janet stuck out her tongue at him.

"OK. My turn!" Jerry McAllister stepped up to the line and whipped the ball at the target.

Janet jumped as the ball slammed into the tarp behind the target. "You just have to *hit* the target," she said. "You don't have to kill it!"

"Who asked you?" Jerry asked. He wound up and slammed another ball into the tarp. "Geez!" he cried, stomping his foot.

Janet laughed. "That was, like, a mile away, Jerry," she said. "Maybe if you'd treat the ball with a little more respect, you'd be able to hit the target."

Jerry narrowed his eyes at the target and slowly brought his arm back. Whack!

Miss again! His turn was over.

Janet glanced once more at the clock. "Well, it looks like the fair's going to be closing in about ten minutes. I think it's time to start cleaning up," she said as she started for the ladder.

"Just a minute." Donald Zwerdling stepped up to the line. He held up a purple ticket. "You can't close up while I've still got a ticket."

Janet snorted. "*You!*" she cried. Donald Zwerdling had to be the most uncoordinated imp to ever set foot in Sweet Valley Middle School. "You couldn't hit the target if it was two inches in front of your face," Janet continued. "Why don't you just save us all the embarrassment and forget it?"

Donald shook his head. "No way. I paid my money like everyone else. And I demand my turn!"

"It *is* only fair," Mary said.

"Oh, all right." Janet sighed. "Let's just get this over with."

Donald took a ball from Mandy. He stretched out his arm and stared down the length of it as if he was really taking aim.

Janet rolled her eyes. "Just throw it, Zwerdling," she said.

Donald's first throw banked off the basketball backboard at the free-shot booth next door. "Hey!" Tim Davis yelled as he picked up the baseball. "You almost hit me!"

"Sorry," Donald yelled back.

Janet snickered. She'd *warned* him to save himself the embarrassment.

Tim threw the ball back to the Unicorns, and Tamara stepped forward to catch it. She handed it to Donald.

"Let's see if you can keep the ball over on our side this time," Janet said.

Donald pointed the ball toward the target and stared down his arm again. He drew back and threw. This time he managed to hit the tarp.

Janet sighed. At least this was almost over. She should be thankful it was someone like Donald Zwerdling at the line. Anybody else probably had half a chance at hitting the target and dropping her into the liquid Jell-O.

Donald aimed his final ball and let it go.

Ding!

No! Janet's eyes grew wide with panic as she felt the chair give out from under her. She grasped at the sideboard, but there was no way she could stop herself from splashing into the purple liquid.

"Hooray!"

"Way to go, Donald!"

Janet felt the anger bubble inside her as she struggled to her feet. She shook her hair and spit out the sugary purple water. She wiped her face and glared at the cheering crowd.

Donald Zwerdling had the goofiest grin on his face as he pointed and laughed at her.

"I'll get you for this, Zwerdling!" Janet yelled. "If it's the last thing I do, I'll get you!"

Fourteen

"That's it!" Jessica said. "No more fortune-telling. I'm hanging it up as a psychic."

"I can't tell you how glad I am to hear that!" Elizabeth said as she toweled off her hair. The twins were in their bathroom, cleaning up after the fair. The tub and sink were speckled with flakes of red, yellow, and blue paint. Dirty clothes and towels lay in a heap on the floor.

"From now on I'm keeping my psychic predictions to myself," Jessica went on as she leaned in to the mirror and dabbed some cold cream on her nose.

Elizabeth stared wide-eyed at Jessica's reflection in the mirror. "Keeping them to yourself?" she repeated. "You mean you still think you're psychic?"

Jessica's eyes twinkled. "When you've got a gift, Lizzie, it doesn't just disappear, you know," she told her sister. "And my psychic abilities told me all along that the fair was going to be a huge success."

Elizbeth grinned. "It was, wasn't it? Ms. Luster said we made all kinds of money. We'll probably be able to get some CD-ROM stuff for the library."

"I'm not talking about the library," Jessica said. "I'm talking about when Janet landed in that disgusting pool of . . . *whatever* it was! Wasn't that just the greatest moment of the entire fair?"

Elizabeth giggled. "That was pretty funny," she agreed. "And I have to say, Janet had it coming after she made all the other Unicorns sit up in that dunking chair while she snuck around like the slimy little weasel she is."

Jessica's mouth dropped open. "For such a nice person, you *do* have an interesting way of putting things sometimes."

Elizabeth smiled in response. "I'm a journalist. I call it like I see it."

"Congratulations to the students at Sweet Valley Middle School," Mr. Clark said at Monday morning's assembly.

Jessica was sitting between her sister and Aaron Dallas in a row behind the Unicorns, eager to hear what Mr. Clark would say about the school fair.

"I see he got his family emergency taken care of," Janet muttered.

"Shhh!" Jessica hissed. "I want to hear how much we made."

"I want to hear who won the free pizza for the most overdue library book," Aaron Dallas said. He sat with his fingers, arms, and legs crossed.

"I am pleased to announce that, as a whole, you

raised more than four hundred dollars for the library," Mr. Clark said.

"Yeah! Hooray!" kids yelled as they clapped their hands and stomped their feet.

"In particular, I'd like to recognize the Unicorn Club for their contributions. Their dunk tank raised almost one hundred dollars, which is more than any other booth raised."

Jessica watched as Mandy and Mary gave each other a high five.

"No thanks to you, Mr. Clark," Janet grumbled.

"Yeah, yeah, get to the pizza prize!" Aaron said impatiently.

"Next I'd like to recognize Jessica Wakefield for her contribution. Her fortune-telling booth raised more than forty dollars for the library, which is the second-highest amount raised by a single booth."

"Yes!" Jessica whispered.

"Way to go, Jess!" Elizabeth patted her on the back.

"And last, but not least . . . the prize for the most overdue library book," Mr. Clark went on.

"Please! Please! Please! Please! Please!" Aaron got down on his hands and knees and raised his crossed fingers.

"Mrs. Janice Dallas!" Mr. Clark announced. "For the book *Black Beauty*, which was due in 1962."

"All right!" Aaron yelled as he jumped up and down. "My grandma won the pizza!"

Janet turned around and looked at Jessica. "And it looks like *we* beat *you*," she said smugly.

Jessica tossed her hair. "Yeah, but it took nine of you to raise that much money. If there were nine of me telling fortunes, we would've raised way more money than you did."

Janet rolled her eyes. "If there were nine of you, the world would be a very scary place!"

"Speaking of scary, look!" Ellen pointed at the side door. Coach Cassels had Brian Boyd by the arm and was leading him out of the auditorium. Neither of them looked very happy.

"I wonder what Brian did now?" Lila said.

"Boy, he's always in trouble for something," Jessica whispered.

"Yeah," Elizabeth agreed. "I wonder what his problem is?"

What's the matter with Brian Boyd? Find out in Sweet Valley Twins #94, Don't Talk to Brian.

Bantam Books in the SWEET VALLEY TWINS series.
Ask your bookseller for the books you have missed.

Sweet Valley Twins Super Editions

Sweet Valley Twins Super Chiller Editions

Sweet Valley Twins Magna Editions

SIGN UP FOR THE SWEET VALLEY HIGH® FAN CLUB!

Hey, girls! Get all the gossip on Sweet Valley High's® most popular teenagers when you join our fantastic Fan Club! As a member, you'll get all of this really cool stuff:

- Membership Card with your own personal Fan Club ID number
- A Sweet Valley High® Secret Treasure Box
- Sweet Valley High® Stationery
- Official Fan Club Pencil (for secret note writing!)
- Three Bookmarks
- A "Members Only" Door Hanger
- Two Skeins of J. & P. Coats® Embroidery Floss with flower barrette instruction leaflet
- Two editions of *The Oracle* newsletter
- Plus exclusive Sweet Valley High® product offers, special savings, contests, and much more!

Be the first to find out what Jessica & Elizabeth Wakefield are up to by joining the Sweet Valley High® Fan Club for the one-year membership fee of only $6.25 each for U.S. residents, $8.25 for Canadian residents (U.S. currency). Includes shipping & handling.

Send a check or money order (do not send cash) made payable to "Sweet Valley High® Fan Club" along with this form to:

SWEET VALLEY HIGH® FAN CLUB, BOX 3919-B, SCHAUMBURG, IL 60168-3919

NAME_____
(Please print clearly)

ADDRESS_____

CITY_____ STATE _____ ZIP_____
(Required)

AGE_____ BIRTHDAY_____ /_____ /_____

Offer good while supplies last. Allow 6-8 weeks after check clearance for delivery. Addresses without ZIP codes cannot be honored. Offer good in USA & Canada only. Void where prohibited by law.
©1993 by Francine Pascal   LCI-1383-123